GIRLS' Weekend in VEGAS

Four friends, four dream weddings!

On a girly weekend in Las Vegas, best friends
Alex, Molly, Serena and Jayne are supposed to
just have fun and forget men—but they end up
meeting their perfect matches! Will the love
they find in Vegas stay in Vegas?

Find out in this sassy, fun and wildly romantic
miniseries all about love and friendship!

S0-AYW-517

Dear Reader,

I had great fun writing this continuity with the other authors, and creating characters who are dealing with the aftermath of one crazy night. We've all had a crazy night (or two!) and I think we can all relate to Molly and Linc's story.

I also like the whole idea of taking a gamble on love. Love is a risk, no matter how you come across it in your life or who with. You're opening your heart, opening your soul to another person, and that means you run the risk of two outcomes—happiness or hurt. Being a romance author, I'm always rooting for the first one. I believe in taking those risks and then seeing how that gamble pays off. Molly and Linc took a risk, and then another when they get back together to deal with the consequences of their one crazy night.

The other thing these books are about is friendship. The authors I wrote this continuity with are some great friends of mine in real life, and I was honored to be a part of this series with them. They're the kind of women you could sit down and have a cup of coffee with, and before you know it, four hours have passed while you've been chatting.

So grab a cup of java for yourself, sit down and enjoy Molly and Linc's story!

Thanks for reading, and as always, feel free to visit my Web site, www.shirleyjump.com, or write to me at P.O. Box 5126, Fort Wayne, IN 46895. I always love to hear from readers!

Shirley

SHIRLEY JUMP

Vegas Pregnancy Surprise

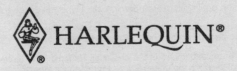

TORONTO • NEW YORK • LONDON
AMSTERDAM • PARIS • SYDNEY • HAMBURG
STOCKHOLM • ATHENS • TOKYO • MILAN • MADRID
PRAGUE • WARSAW • BUDAPEST • AUCKLAND

Recycling programs
for this product may
not exist in your area.

ISBN-13: 978-0-373-17671-7

VEGAS PREGNANCY SURPRISE

First North American Publication 2010.

Copyright © 2010 by Shirley Kawa-Jump, LLC.

Printed in U.S.A.

New York Times bestselling author **Shirley Jump** didn't have the willpower to diet, or the talent to master under-eye concealer, so she bowed out of a career in television and opted instead for a career where she could be paid to eat at her desk—writing. At first, seeking revenge on her children for their grocery-store tantrums, she sold embarrassing essays about them to anthologies. However, it wasn't enough to feed her growing addiction to writing. So she turned to the world of romance novels, where messes are (usually) cleaned up before The End. In the worlds Shirley gets to create and control, the children listen to their parents, the husbands always remember holidays and the housework is magically done by elves. Though she's thrilled to see her books in stores around the world, Shirley mostly writes because it gives her an excuse to avoid cleaning the toilets and helps feed her shoe habit. To learn more, visit her Web site at www.shirleyjump.com.

Praise for Shirley Jump:

"Shirley Jump's *Miracle on Christmas Eve* has a solid plot and [an] involving conflict, and the characters are wonderful."
—*RT Book Reviews*

About *Sweetheart Lost and Found*
"This tale of rekindled love is right on target;
a delightful start to this uplifting, marriage-oriented series
[The Wedding Planners]."
—*Library Journal*.com

About *New York Times* bestselling anthology *Sugar and Spice*
"Jump's office romance gives the collection a kick,
with fiery writing."
—*Publishers Weekly*.com

CHAPTER ONE

Two pink lines.

Molly Hunter stared for a good thirty seconds at the long white stick displaying its message like a beacon atop her peach tile bathroom counter. Put it down, picked it up, stared at the double pink message some more.

It couldn't be. Had to be…impossible.

Nausea sent her stomach on a renewed roll and pitch, as if daring her to disagree. For the past couple of weeks she'd been waking up nauseous, tired, but with three of her summer school students out sick over the last month with the flu, she'd attributed her touchy stomach to them. Not to—

Oh, God. To that night in Vegas.

Two months ago. Had it been that long? How could she not have noticed?

Easy. She didn't have a boyfriend, or a husband, and the chances of her getting pregnant were slim to none. Except this time Slim had apparently been an overachiever.

Her mind rocketed back to the bar, to a gorgeous man with blue eyes and dark hair. A man she knew only by his first name.

Linc.

"No last names."

"No commitments."
"Nothing but tonight."

One crazy, insane night when Molly Hunter, who never did anything without a plan, without thinking things through, had thrown caution to the wind, and let a nearly electric attraction rule her every thought.

Ever since that night, she'd done her best to try to forget the intoxicating man she'd met in Vegas, and she'd thought she'd done a pretty good job of it. He'd been a momentary attraction, a crazy aberration in her life, and even though every once in a while her thoughts drifted to where he might be or whether he was thinking about her, she told herself leaving that one-night stand where it was—in the back of her thoughts as a delicious one-night memory— was the best thing all around.

After all, she was a kindergarten teacher, who did nothing more exciting than teach remedial English to high schoolers in the summer. A conservative woman in every sense of the word. She never did anything remotely like that.

Well, *never* wasn't exactly the right term. Almost never!

She'd gone to Vegas with one purpose—to help her good friend Jayne Cavendish forget about the devastating end of her engagement to Rich Strickland. The four friends— Molly, Jayne, Alex Lowell and Serena Warren—had planned a girls' weekend of manicures, martinis and memories.

They'd done just that the first night, but then the second night they'd been more adventurous, going off in their own directions. For some of them, that time apart had clearly resulted in a bit of trouble.

For Molly—a lot of trouble. She gave the stick a solid shake, then looked at it again. Still two pink lines.

You're pregnant! those lines screamed in their happy, friendly pastel color.

Yeah, and totally unprepared for this life-changing event, her mind shouted back.

Oh, God. What was she going to do? What *on earth* was she going to do?

"Hello! Molly?"

Her mother's bright, cheery voice carried through Molly's San Diego bungalow. Molly scooped the pregnancy test, the box and wrapper and hurried to bury them all in the white wicker trash basket, shoving several tissues on top. She emerged from the bathroom, tightening the belt of her white terrycloth robe as she crossed into the kitchen. Rocky, her Jack Russell mix, trotted along at her heels, eying her every few steps and wagging his tail. "Mom. What brings you by so early?" She reached for the dog food, then the small stainless steel bowl beside the canister.

She avoided her mother's inquisitive gaze. Hoping her face didn't betray a worried flush. She could only hope that Jayne wouldn't wake up any time soon. She couldn't deal with her temporary roommate's questions, too, especially since Jayne had been there that weekend.

Molly ran a hand through her hair. Had she really done that? Been so…careless? Was she really…pregnant?

"Early?" Cynthia Hunter gaped at her daughter. "Goodness, Molly. It's ten after eight."

Molly paused in filling Rocky's bowl. "That late? Already?" She hurried to put the bowl on the floor. Rocky scrambled after the kibble, his tail now in overdrive. "I have to get out of here."

"But, Molly, I thought we'd sit down and chat. Your summer school session ended yesterday. Don't you have plenty of time to—?"

"Sorry, no!" Molly had already spun on her heel and headed toward her bedroom. She'd spent too much time in the bathroom, staring at that stupid stick, as if looking at the lines would make the result any different. She tossed her robe on the unmade, sleep-rumpled bed—she'd have to let that housekeeping detail go for today, even though it would bug her—then threw open her closet and grabbed the first outfit she saw. Gray poplin slacks, a short-sleeved lilac sweater set and black kitten heels.

Two quick light raps sounded on Molly's bedroom door. "Do you want breakfast, honey? I can make you some poached eggs."

The thought nearly made Molly rush to the bathroom again. "No. No, thanks, Mom." She slid the sweater over her head, buttoned her slacks and stepped into the shoes. A quick brush through her hair, a touch of makeup on her face, and she was done—or at least close enough to pass muster.

Molly headed out of her bedroom, running through a mental list as she walked. She really didn't need to bring anything to today's meeting, but she liked to be prepared just in case. She'd grab that binder filled with her ideas for next year's curriculum changes. Oh, and the grant she was working on to expand the reading program. Rumor had it there were going to be cutbacks at Washington Elementary. Molly wanted to be sure not be caught in that if the rumors were true.

She was still running through her day when she rounded the corner—and nearly collided with Jayne. "Oh, sorry!"

Jayne laughed and brushed a few stray tendrils of her short chestnut hair off her forehead. "No problem. You're in a hurry this morning. Are you leaving early for the meeting with administration?"

Molly nodded.

Jayne assessed her. "Are you nervous? You don't look like yourself." The two of them headed into the living room, with Molly feeling caught between the inquisitive eyes of her mother and Jayne at the same time. How on earth was she going to hide this secret?

Well, she had to. She didn't even know anything for sure. Not yet.

"No." Molly let out a sigh. "Yes."

"You'll do fine," Cynthia said.

"It's not that, Mom." Molly crossed to the small desk in her living room, gathered up the binder holding the curriculum and the folder with the grant materials, then put both into her dark brown leather tote bag. "The budget is what the budget is. If there's funding for a second kindergarten class this year, then I'll have a job. And if there isn't...."

"You won't. But I'm sure it'll be fine," her mother said.

Jayne dittoed her support.

Molly nodded. She couldn't imagine not working at Washington Elementary School and seeing another flock of kindergarteners in the fall. Their inquisitive faces, blossoming like spring flowers when they learned the basics, from their alphabet to simple addition. She loved her job—and couldn't picture herself doing anything else. She'd done the same thing, day in and day out, for years, and that was exactly how she liked her life.

If that was so, then why had she been so eager to let loose that one night? To act as if she were someone else?

A psychologist would probably say it was because she was seeking to fill a void in herself. Molly brushed that thought aside. The night had been an aberration, nothing more. She had no "voids" in her life to fill. She was fine.

She'd been in Vegas merely to support Jayne, who'd been going through a rough patch. That was all.

"You look pale," Cynthia said, taking a step forward and laying a hand on her daughter's forehead. "Not like yourself. Didn't you say a summer flu bug was going around? Maybe you caught it."

She'd caught something all right.

"You do look a little run down, Moll," Jayne put in.

"I'm tired. That's all." No way was she going to tell her mother or her friend about the pregnancy test, not until she'd seen a doctor. Those tests could be wrong, couldn't they?

After two months? the little voice whispered. *What, did you fail Health class?*

Her mother pursed her lips. "Well, if you ask me, you haven't been taking proper care of yourself since you and Doug had that…pause in your relationship."

Molly opened the back door, let Rocky into the fenced yard, then turned around to face her mother. Jayne busied herself making coffee, staying out of the familiar mother-daughter argument. "Mom, it wasn't a *pause*. We're divorced."

Cynthia shook her head. "I still think you can—"

"No. We can't."

Her mother's lips pursed even more, but she didn't say anything.

Molly let out a sigh, but didn't pursue the argument. In Cynthia's eyes, Douglas Wyndham could do no wrong. She'd seen him as the perfect son-in-law, the doctor who was "going places."

The only problem? The places he wanted to go, and the places Molly wanted to go were on two polar sides of the life spectrum. And now—

Well, she wasn't going to think about it, she resolved yet again. She didn't know for sure if those pink lines were even right. She'd call the doctor and try to get an appointment for right after her meeting. Then she'd know for sure.

Know *what*, though? That she had possibly made the

biggest mistake of her life that night? She, Molly Hunter, the woman who lived life so straight and narrow she might as well be a ruler?

"Molly, I still think—"

"Can I get you some coffee, Mrs. Hunter?" Jayne asked. Molly flashed her friend a relieved smile for the subject-change.

Rocky scratched at the screen door, so Molly let him in, fished his favorite chew toy out from under the refrigerator, and gave him one last pat. She grabbed her purse from the hall table, and dug inside for her sunglasses. "I'm sorry I don't have time to stay and chat, Mom. I wanted to get to the meeting early."

"At least Rocky here is glad to see me." Her mother bent down and patted Rocky on the head. His tail beat a steady pattern against her leg.

Molly headed for the front door, opened it, and waited for her mother to follow. "I'll call you after the meeting. Promise."

"Aren't you forgetting something?"

Molly glanced down at the tote bag, then back at Rocky, who was happily gnawing on his rubber bone. "Uh, I don't think so."

"Your keys?" Cynthia pointed at the hall table. "Goodness, Molly, you *are* forgetful today." She reached out, put a palm on Molly's forehead. "Are you sure you're feeling all right?"

"I'm fine." Except for this little baby thing. Possibly.

"You look a little peaked."

"Mom, no one says peaked anymore," Molly said, dashing over to grab her keys before returning to the door. "And I'm just fine. Really."

"Jayne," Cynthia said, turning to the other woman as she entered the foyer. "Don't you think Molly looks peaked?"

Jayne sent Molly a smile that said she understood meddlesome mothers. "If she's pale, Mrs. Hunter, I'm sure it's just because she's been too busy to get outside and putter around in her garden."

Molly mouthed a silent thank you Jayne's way.

A twinge of guilt ran through Molly. She hadn't told Jayne—or any of her friends who had been with her that weekend in Vegas—about what had happened that night. It had been so out of character, such an insane decision, and Molly just couldn't seem to find the words to explain her irrational choice. At twenty-eight, she should know better, for Pete's sake, than to let her hormones do the thinking for her. But that night...

That night she hadn't done much thinking at all.

She thought of the two pink lines and realized if they were right, she was going to have to find some words pretty soon.

Cynthia gave a dubious shrug. "If you say so."

Jayne pressed a shiny silver travel mug into Molly's hands. "Here. This'll get you through the morning."

Molly grinned. "Thanks." She accepted the coffee, not telling Jayne she wasn't sure she should be having all that caffeine.

"Hey, making coffee is the least I can do for you putting up with me all this time."

"You didn't have to do that." Molly smiled. "You're a great roommate, Jayne. I love having you here." And she had. Ever since Jayne Cavendish had moved in two months ago, every day had been fun. She hadn't minded one bit having one of her best friends to fill the empty spaces in the tiny bungalow, and she suspected Jayne, who was still nursing a broken heart, was happy for the company, too.

Molly's heart went out to Jayne. She understood what it was like to see your dreams for happily-ever-after dashed. It was partly why Molly had thought going to Vegas that weekend with Jayne, Alex and Serena would be just the right medicine to help Jayne forget her fiancé's betrayal. The four of them had intended to have one crazy, fun, girls-only weekend filled with lots of laughs and incredible memories.

They'd gotten more than they bargained for, that was for sure. Alex had ended up staying in Vegas to run Wyatt McKendrick's hotel—and ended up falling in love with the handsome hotelier. Serena, who had impetuously married Jonas Benjamin on that wild weekend, had also stayed in Vegas and so far had stayed married, though she hadn't said much about life with her politician husband. Molly missed her friends desperately, and except for one weekend when Wyatt had brought all the friends together for a quick lunch and shopping visit, they'd had to keep in virtual touch via texts, online chats and phone calls.

Jayne gave Molly a quick hug, wished her luck at her meeting, then told her she was heading inside. "I have to get ready for work. Maybe we'll get pizza tonight and rent a couple movies."

"Sounds great." Except for the pizza part, which had Molly's stomach rebelling yet again. After Jayne left, Molly opened the front door and gestured for her mother to leave first. But Cynthia held her ground. "Mom, I have to get to that meeting."

Her mother smiled, the kind of smile that told Molly a conversation was coming she didn't want to hear. "If you want, I could call Douglas…?"

"You don't have to call Doug."

"Molly, really, I think you're being awfully hard on him. Can't you two work it out?"

Work out what? She and Doug had been divorced for

over two years now, and still her mother thought resurrecting her failed marriage was as simple as picking up the phone and arranging a dinner date. She didn't seem to understand the arguments that had driven a wedge between Doug and her, the differences in everything from the way they viewed the world to the future they envisioned together.

She'd been so naïve when she'd married Doug. She was swept off her feet by his charm, the way he took care of every little detail, making her busy life suddenly seem easy. At first, it was simple to fall into Doug's regimented world, to let him make the decisions. Then, too late, she'd realized that he had no intentions of relaxing the rigid rules by which he lived. The man who had seemed so organized and under control she now saw as unyielding and closed off to the full life of children. The life that she wanted.

If she ever got married again—and that if was so big it topped Mt. Everest—she'd give the event weeks, maybe months of careful thought. No rushing in, no thinking with her hormones instead of her brains.

She'd be smart. Not infatuated. Ever again.

"Doug is miserable, you know," her mother added, then she sighed. "I just want you to be happy, like your father and I were." Her mother's eyes misted at the mention of Molly's late father.

"I am happy, Mom."

"Being alone?" Cynthia shook her head. "How?"

Molly realized then that her mother's concern stemmed more from her own difficulties dealing with the loss of her husband eighteen months ago than worry about the demise of Molly's marriage. "You get involved, Mom. Join that bridge club you've been talking about. Go to the book club at the library."

Cynthia looked away.

"Mom…"

"They're reading *Wuthering Heights* this month," she said softly.

"You love Brontë."

Cynthia turned back to her daughter. "Are you sure you're feeling all right?" she said instead, retreating to the safety of playing mother hen. "If you want, I can stay."

Molly's stomach was rebelling, and the mere thought of making the six-mile drive to work had her wishing she could turn right around and head back to bed, but she refused to tell her mother that. "Go to the book club meeting, Mom. I'm fine. I'll call you later." She pressed a kiss to her mother's cheek, inhaling her familiar scent. "I promise."

Then she got in the car, and left, before her mother could finish the sentence she was beginning to sputter. Molly sent Cynthia a wave, then headed down the driveway and off to work.

Only eight-fifteen. At least an hour and a half until her meeting with the administration was over and she could get into Dr. Carter's office. The day had barely begun and already, she could swear it had lasted a year.

"I know what I want, and that isn't it." Lincoln Curtis slid the portfolio across the polished mahogany table to the team of architects sitting on the other side like ducks in a row. The three men had on nearly identical navy blue suits and red ties of varying patterns, as if dressing in unison was a requirement for working at King Architecture.

That had to explain why Lincoln hated the design. Uninspired in attire, uninspired in thinking.

"Sir, we can draw a new—"

"I'm done. You're done." Lincoln rose. "Thank you for your time." He headed out of the conference room, trailed by Conner Paulson, the CFO for Curtis Systems, the security software company Lincoln and his brother had started twelve years ago in the basement of their parents' home. In one year, the two Curtis brothers had taken Curtis Systems from an idea to a company servicing Fortune 500 firms. Five years later, they were turning down multi-million-dollar buyout offers from international software giants. Lincoln, the elder, had been the CEO, while Marcus, two years younger, had been the vice president.

Now he had the company he'd always dreamed of, one that was even bigger than he'd dreamed. Perfect in every respect—

Except for the empty office beside his own. The one that mocked the very success Linc had worked so hard to build. But now he knew nothing else, and had nothing else. So the company got all of Lincoln Curtis, and then some.

"The architects gave you exactly what you said you wanted," Conner said, falling into stride beside Lincoln as they headed down the wide hallway toward Lincoln's office. "What's changed since you met with them last quarter and now?"

"Nothing."

Conner snorted. "Are you kidding me? Everything's different about you lately."

Lincoln stopped. "What do you mean?"

"Don't tell me you're going to stick to the same song you've been giving me for the last two months. That nothing's on your mind. That you're just fine." Conner mocked talking with his hand. "This is me, Linc. I've known you since first grade. And you are so far from fine you're on another planet."

"What's that supposed to mean?"

Conner sighed. "Listen, I wouldn't say this if I wasn't

your best friend, and hadn't known you forever. But for years you've been…"

"What?" Lincoln prodded.

"Well, you took your brother's death pretty hard. We all did," Conner added. "But you especially. And I don't blame you. If I'd been there—"

"Do we need to have this conversation?"

Conner opened his mouth, shut it again. "No."

"Good."

"All I'm saying is that for a long time you've been a robot. Getting the job done, working like a maniac. Except for that one vacation—"

"I thought we weren't having this conversation."

"Then after that…" Conner paused, his gaze softening in sympathy. "Afterwards, you went back to being the same old Linc. No one could blame you, really, but—"

"Drop it," Linc said, his voice a warning. Conner was his best friend, but even with him Linc didn't journey back to that day three years ago.

Conner let out a gust that voiced concession to the change of topic. "Lately…I don't know, you just seem to have a new attitude. A good one, I might add. Like with the idea you proposed a couple months ago about that software for kids—"

"An idea that you and the other suits shot down if I remember right," Linc pointed out. "And you were right. I shouldn't be running off, pursuing crazy ideas that could just end up draining company resources instead of adding to the coffers."

For a moment, he'd thought maybe—

Maybe he could bring back something he'd lost by digging up a bit of the past. So he'd floated the idea, then come to his senses when the number crunchers smacked it down.

"Hey, maybe someday that program can work, Linc, sure, but honestly, I don't see you finding the time for anything more. Don't you agree?" Conner laid a hand on his arm. "You're the most tightly scheduled guy I know. Not to mention…"

"What?" Linc asked when Conner didn't finish.

"As much as I think it would be terrific for you to step out of your comfort zone of memos, day planners and task lists, I'm just not sure launching a kid-oriented product like that is up your particular alley."

"Because I'm not fun," Linc replied, reading the words Conner wasn't speaking.

"Let's just say when I'm looking for a partner in crime for hosting a wild party, your name isn't at the top of my list." Conner grinned. "But I'd still send you an invitation."

Linc let out a short laugh. If only Conner knew how far Linc had stepped out of his world of schedules and memos that night two months ago.

In his mind, he saw the image of Molly—Linc didn't know her last name, by agreement with both of them—smiling up at him as she lay back on the pale cream-colored sheets of the Bellagio's luxurious king-sized bed. Her dark brown hair tumbling around her shoulders, her green eyes wide and sparkling, her lithe body still tempting even after he'd spent so many exquisite moments exploring, tasting and enjoying every inch.

For one night, Linc had been someone other than himself.

"What made you propose the idea in the first place?" Conner asked. "It just came out of the blue."

They had reached the glass corridor that connected the twin towers of Curtis Systems, and provided a stunning view of downtown Vegas. On either side of him, the city flashed a constant rainbowed heartbeat of activity. "It's something I've been kicking around for years."

A lie. But telling the truth meant opening wounds Linc preferred not to open.

Two months ago he'd looked at the date and realized it was his brother's birthday. If he had lived, Marcus would have been twenty-six this year.

And Linc hadn't moved one inch closer in all those years to finishing the software program that had been the genesis of everything for Curtis Systems. The first dream he and his brother had shared.

He'd sat in his empty apartment for hours, revisiting past mistakes and regrets. And then, finally, spurred by nostalgia, regrets or maybe something more, he'd gone out, headed to one of the bars in Vegas—

And ended up sleeping with a woman he barely knew.

"There's something else, though," Conner said. "Something you're not telling me."

Linc met his friend's inquisitive stare. "I met someone."

A flicker of surprise flashed across Conner's face. "Great. You've been alone too long. So who is she? And why didn't you bring her to the benefit dinner last week?" Conner flashed him a grin. "You hiding her in your apartment?"

"I don't know where she is. I don't even know her last name. And that's where I'm leaving things."

That one night with Molly was enough. The last thing he needed was a relationship, not just because of the distraction it would provide, but because of the expectations involved. A woman in his life would want time. Energy. And that would divide him between the company and his personal life. Right now, that was a division problem he couldn't solve.

Conner stumbled to a stop. He grabbed Lincoln's arm. "You had a one-night stand? *You?*"

"It wasn't just a one-night stand. It was…" Lincoln searched for the words to describe that night two months ago. The intoxicating magic of the woman he had met, how she had brought out a side of him he had thought he'd lost three years ago, how she had made him forget—

Forget who he was. Forget the burdens he'd carried for so long. Forget his guilt, his regrets. Forget the Curtis empire, and its expectations. For one night, he could just…be.

"It was so much more," Lincoln finished. "At least until I got back to reality."

In the two months since he'd seen Molly, he had tried to forget her by pouring himself into his work. By tightening an already tight schedule, filling already full days. Developing expanded product lines, pushing his team to create newer and more improved systems than the company already had.

Yet a part of him kept going back to that night, to those questions neither of them had asked, because they'd agreed never to know the answers. Was that all this was? A puzzle he needed to solve?

"Either way, it doesn't matter. The night's over. In the past." As he said the words, he cemented his resolve to keep the memory there. He had no room for a relationship right now.

He, of all people, could not afford a distraction like that. He had only to look at the empty office beside his own to remember why.

"If it's so 'in the past,'" Conner said, using air quotes, "then why is she still on your mind?"

"She's not." Linc scowled.

Conner looked at Linc. And chuckled. "Uh-huh."

Lincoln gazed out over the city, at the miles and miles of brightly lit buildings, stucco-coated homes, and beyond that, the vast, empty desert. Vegas stuck out among all the nothingness like a wild rose in a field of plain, practical wheat. How apropos, really, of the way he lived his personal life. That one night had been an aberration—and that was the way it would stay.

Lincoln Curtis lived his life in straight lines. It was the only way he knew to maintain control. To keep himself from thinking of the promises he'd made so many years ago. Promises he had broken.

Linc pivoted away from the window and faced Conner. "The past is over, Conner. I'm all about focusing on the future. And my future is contained inside this business."

CHAPTER TWO

MOLLY sat in her car and cried.

No job. No husband for support. No possibility of either in the near future.

And a baby on the way.

If she could have written a script for her life, she couldn't have imagined a worse ending for this day. Within two hours, her entire world had been turned upside down.

Lack of funding...positions cut...difficult decision to make...we're so sorry...wish you well...

She could still see the faces of the administration officials as they told her they were letting her go, with the promise that if funding improved, she would be the first kindergarten teacher hired back—

Next fall.

From there, she'd gone to her doctor's office, sure he'd tell her she'd misread the pink lines, or bought a faulty kit, or had a hormonal spike. Instead, Dr. Carter had walked back into the examination room, a wide smile on his face. "Wonderful news, Molly. You're pregnant!"

She'd started to cry. She'd cried while he wrote her a prescription for prenatal vitamins, while she made her next appointment, and all the way home.

Oh, God. What was she going to do? How was she going to deal with this?

It still didn't seem real. Didn't seem possible. The words *you're pregnant* swirled again in her head, and sounded like they had been spoken to someone else.

Pregnant.

Now she sat in her driveway, allowed the last few tears to fall, then wiped her face and made some decisions.

Number one. She needed a job. She had a mortgage, and even though Jayne was paying rent, without the regular income from teaching, very soon there wasn't going to be enough money to pay all the bills. Not to mention the need for health insurance to cover her pregnancy. In seven months, Molly would have another life to provide for, and that meant putting aside as much money as she could between here and then.

Another life.

The words hit her again, and she still couldn't quite comprehend her situation. A baby.

The one thing she had dreamed about for so many years, imagined having when she'd married Doug—

But then Doug had made it infinitely clear children weren't on his agenda, not now, not later, not ever. That had been the beginning of the end for them, the moment when she'd realized she'd married a man who didn't share any of her dreams for the future.

Now she had the future she wanted. Except she was alone. And about to become penniless. Not the dream she'd envisioned. How could she, of all people, have ended up in this position?

She'd always been so careful with her life, so conservative. The one time she'd stepped out of those boundaries she'd ended up pregnant, alone and unemployed.

Boy, karma had a heck of a sense of humor.

Molly sighed. She reached for another tissue in her purse and faced issue number two.

The baby's father.

She might not want to see him again, might want to pretend that night in Vegas never happened, but she couldn't.

She had to tell him. Somehow. And sometime in the next few months.

How would Linc react? She didn't know him well enough to predict how he ordered his coffee in the morning, much less something as huge as this.

Oh, what had she done?

Either way, whether he wanted anything to do with the baby or not, she had to know, if only for the baby's sake, who this man was. What if there was a medical problem? What if their child asked her a question someday down the road?

She thought back to that crazy, heady night two months ago. Did Linc ever think of her? Did he ever wonder whether there had been consequences to their temporary insanity? If he saw her again, what would he do? Say? He'd probably forgotten all about her, and if he saw her again wouldn't even remember her name, much less what had happened between them.

With a man that handsome, in a city like Las Vegas, the chances were good that he had dozens of women in his life. Molly could have just been one more in a long string of quick dates.

Or not.

She had no idea what kind of man he really was because they'd agreed to keep everything easy, fun. No personal details, no heart-to-heart connections, no relationship-building.

Did she want to see him again? That was a bigger question. Did she really want to face her dumbest decision again? No.

But wanting to and *having* to were two totally different things.

And finally, decision number three.

She needed to keep this entire situation to herself for as long as possible, until she had it all figured out. She could just imagine her mother's reaction—she'd be calling Doug and trying to fix Molly back up with her ex-husband, regardless of whether the two of them should be together or not or whether he wanted anything to do with children. Never mind a child that wasn't even his.

Yeah, she was not going to tell anyone about this. Not until she had to.

Molly got out of her car and headed into the house. Rocky greeted her with the same enthusiasm as always, licking, barking, jumping all over his mistress. She let him out, then went back into the living room to dump her tote bag and purse on the scarred maple coffee table. Jayne was at work, so Molly had the house to herself and had some more time to process the day. Thank goodness.

As she passed her desk in the corner of the living room, she glanced at her desktop computer. Her gaze strayed to the stack of software piled beside the monitor.

Software.

Linc.

That night in the bar.

No…that was a crazy idea. Absolutely crazy. One that could lead to heartbreak, especially if Linc said he didn't remember her, or their conversation about the software product he wanted to launch. Then again, could the idea be any crazier than the one that had gotten her into this situation in the first place?

* * *

The dry Vegas air slammed into Molly as soon as she got out of the taxicab. The August heat seemed to weigh on her, like a thick, suffocating blanket. Dry or not—it was hot.

"Are you sure this is the right place?" she asked the cab driver.

The older man at the wheel of the car gestured toward the towering glass buildings, twin mirrors of each other, connected by an all-glass skybridge. The building was impressive, with neat linear lines and a clean silver-and-glass exterior, a stark contrast to the colorful noise of the Vegas strip a little ways behind them. "Curtis Systems, yes, ma'am. Can't miss it."

Molly thanked and paid the driver. She stepped into the shadow of the Curtis Systems building, dwarfed by the twenty-plus stories above her. Now that she was finally here, trepidation held her rooted to the spot.

She should go home. Forget the whole idea. Come up with another plan.

Except there wasn't really another plan, at least not one that could solve both the job and getting to know the father of her baby dilemma all at once.

She just hadn't expected that the Linc she met in a bar two months ago was *this* Linc.

When she'd search the Internet for Linc, with what little information she had, she'd come back with two different possibilities for software companies in Las Vegas. There'd been many software companies, of course, but only two that returned results with an employee named Linc. The first was no longer in business—all she'd found had been a weedy lot with a "For Sale" sign. That left Curtis Systems.

The company name had returned hundreds of Google hits, link after link showing the meteoric rise of the company's success. Google hadn't lied. She peered up at the monolith of a building. A success story on a mega level. And, according to the information she'd read on the Internet, Linc didn't just work here—he was the owner and CEO.

The man she'd met, the one who seemed so…normal, so guy-next-door, was the same one at the helm of this massive, multi-national, multi-million-dollar corporation?

Again she considered turning around, heading back to San Diego. Then her hand drifted to her stomach, to the new life growing inside her, and she knew she had to go inside that building.

Not just for the job she needed, but for her baby.

Only two days had passed since she'd taken that first pregnancy test, and already she'd come to call this life "her baby." To picture the tiny boy or girl someday living in the little bungalow on Gull View Lane. And to look forward to that event.

People streamed in and out of the Curtis Systems building. Molly fanned herself, and realized she looked a little strange standing on the sidewalk, just staring up at the skyscraper. She couldn't stand here baking in the heat all day. At least the morning sickness had finally abated today. She strode into the building, across the smooth marble foyer, and up to the granite counter reception desk. A friendly-looking blonde finished transferring a phone call, then shot Molly a smile. "Good morning. Can I help you?"

"I'd like to see Linc…" Molly paused, then pulled his last name together with his first, the two words sounding strange on her tongue. "Lincoln Curtis, please."

"Do you have an appointment?"

"No."

The friendliness quotient dropped a little from the blonde's features. "I'm sorry, miss, but Mr. Curtis is a very busy man. Without an appointment…" She put her hands up, implying it was a lost cause.

Appointment?

How was she supposed to get an appointment? What was she supposed to say? *Hi, I'm the woman you met in a bar for a one-night stand. I really need to see you again, can you spare ten minutes?*

Chances were good he wouldn't even remember that night, not to mention her. How horrible would *that* be?

"I spoke with Mr. Curtis a couple months ago about a possible position with his company," Molly said, partially lying, partially telling the truth. They had talked two months ago, and he had made an offhand comment about her working for him, but she hadn't been sure he was serious. "He said if I was ever in town, I should stop by."

The blonde raised a skeptical eyebrow. "Mr. Curtis said that?"

Molly nodded. Added a smile.

The blonde considered that, giving Molly a visual once-over, as if her icy blue eyes were lie detectors. "Is he expecting you?"

No. "Yes, I believe so."

The blonde assessed Molly again, then turned to her computer and struck a few keys. "According to the schedule I have here, Mr. Curtis should be just finishing up a meeting. He has six minutes until the next one, and then he's booked solid for the rest of the day."

"Are you sure? He doesn't have fifteen free minutes?"

The blonde laughed. "You don't know Mr. Curtis very well. He rarely takes enough time to eat lunch." Then her face softened. "I shouldn't tell you this, but if you head up to his office on the twentieth floor, you might be able to catch him between meetings. If not, see Tracy, his assistant. She can schedule a time for you to speak with him. Like I said, he's a very busy man, so be prepared to wait several days for an appointment."

Molly prayed she wouldn't have to wait days. She didn't want to spend the money on a hotel room, only to have the whole thing not work out. She needed every dime she had, and every day she could get, to be looking for a job. Wasting time waiting on Lincoln Curtis wasn't on her agenda.

"Thank you," Molly said to the receptionist, then headed for the elevators. At first, her steps were light, filled with the thrill of victory. But as the elevator doors opened and she stepped inside, she realized where she was going.

And who she was about to see.

The marble and brass elevator began its upward journey with a soft whirr. Molly's stomach, however, dropped, and her queasiness returned, whether due to nerves or the baby or both. What if Linc didn't remember her? Or said he'd been kidding about the job offer? Or turned out to be married?

Or worse, told her to leave?

She reached out a hand to press another button, any other button, then stopped herself. She had to do this. Had to find a way to tell him about the baby—it was only right.

And more, to satisfy her own lingering curiosity about the man she had met. They'd agreed to keep the night free from connections, but still she wondered about him. About what he was like on a longer-term basis.

What if they'd had two nights? A week? A year?

The elevator shuddered to a stop, and the doors opened on the twentieth floor. Molly took a deep breath, then strode forward. She hesitated in the hall. Right? Left? She should have asked.

"Molly?"

The voice, deep, dark, like good chocolate, hit her as

hard as the memory. Sitting in the bar, intoxicated not by the barely touched mixed drink in front of her, but by the conversation, by the way he looked at her and really seemed to see her. Listen to her.

Molly turned around, and there he was. Linc. Looking exactly—well, almost exactly—like he had that night.

He stood in the hall beside a cherry-paneled door labeled "Conference Room," a second man she barely noticed by his side. All she saw was Linc, wearing a tailored navy suit that on another man would have looked merely handsome. But on Linc, the suit gave him an air of power. At his full six-foot-two height, he commanded the wide hallways of Curtis Systems.

"What are you doing here?" he asked.

Now or never. She took a step forward. "Looking for you."

Surprise lit his features. The man beside him looked from Molly to Linc, then back again, clearly curious. With an almost imperceptible flick of his hand, Linc dismissed the other man, who shot Linc a grin, then said something about a meeting and headed off down the corridor.

"Why?" Linc said, taking a step forward and lowering his voice. "I thought we agreed not to see each other again."

Whatever Hollywood reunion she'd secretly hoped to have, with Linc being glad to see her, deflated in that moment, in the neutral tone in his voice. Molly's hand strayed protectively to her abdomen, and she decided there was no way she was going to drop the pregnancy bombshell. Not now. "You were actually the one who told me to look you up if I ever got to Vegas again. Well, I'm in Vegas…and looking you up."

"I…" He thought a second, and in the flash of that moment she panicked, sure she'd done the wrong thing. "I did. But I had no idea you'd actually take me up on the offer."

She'd come all this way, thinking she could walk into Linc's life, take him up on that job offer he'd thrown out the night they met, tell him about the baby, and in the process get to know him—

And it was all falling apart right before her eyes. The tears that had been a constant companion ever since she'd left the doctor's office threatened again at the back of her eyes, but Molly refused to let them win.

She thought of the baby, and a fierce need to take care of the child to come rose within her. She had to find a job. Immediately. No matter what it took.

Linc had made that offer. She had heard him. This could work.

It *would* work.

"I realize I've just dropped in on you out of the blue," she said, wanting only to get out of there, before the tears won or Linc said something else that fractured her composure, but refusing to give up just yet. "And this might be a bad time, so perhaps we can schedule a time to talk."

"Is there something about that night I should know?" His voice had dropped nearly to a whisper.

Here was her chance to tell him the truth. She opened her mouth to say *I'm pregnant*, then shut it again.

Linc's reaction thus far to her presence hadn't exactly spelled overjoyed. He'd been terse, short. Almost... annoyed. She hadn't really expected the Hollywood reaction—him sweeping her into his arms and kissing her passionately—but something a little more enthusiastic would have done a lot for her peace of mind. The pregnancy had already knocked her off center, and to have Linc react as if she was a fly in his soup—

She didn't need one more stress. Not now. Besides, the last place she wanted to share news like this was in a hall outside a conference room. She'd wait for a better time. One when perhaps Linc had come around to the shock of seeing her again.

Surely that was all it was, shock. Not dismay. Or disappointment.

"No," she said finally. "I was simply taking you up on your offer of a job."

"Job offer?"

Oh, damn. Now he did look confused. She shouldn't have come. Definitely should have stayed in San Diego. But she kept on talking, as if saying *more* would fix an already messy situation. "The one you made about that children's software program you were planning to launch?" Suddenly the space seemed too confined, too hot, and regrets piled on her shoulders heavier than bricks. "But I can see I came at a bad time." Oh, man, now she was repeating herself. "I should just—"

"No, no." He reached for her, but didn't connect. "Let's take this somewhere more…quiet," Linc said. "Have you eaten?"

What was with people trying to feed her? Molly's stomach still had a rebellious streak going strong, made worse by the conversation and her nerves, but she shook her head, if only to escape the clear curiosity running through the other people in the offices around them. And find a way to get out of here. "No, I haven't."

Linc closed the distance between them and put a hand against her back—a light touch, nothing more than a guiding glance, but it set off a firestorm of memories in her. Of being with him in that bar, of the first time he'd touched her—

How they'd danced around, touching, for a half-hour that night, hands and fingers coming close, then drifting away, each of them wanting to make contact, neither daring to be the first, and then she had reached for her drink at the same time he had, and their fingers had collided. An instant electric explosion ignited in Molly, more powerful than any she had ever felt. She'd been a goner from that moment on, captured in Linc's spell.

That same electric explosion, albeit slightly muted by the daylight, the other people and the businesslike surroundings, reignited in Molly as Linc guided her into the elevator. They rode down in silence, two among a dozen other people, then stepped out into the lobby and out of the Curtis Systems building. Once they reached the sidewalk his hand dropped away and a whisper of disappointment ran through her.

She shook it off. She wasn't here to start a relationship with Lincoln Curtis. Under no circumstances did she want that. She had enough on her plate to deal with right now. Besides, she hardly knew the man. She couldn't base any rational decisions on one night—made after a few drinks and a lot of hormones.

Not to mention, judging by his reaction at her sudden appearance, he wasn't interested in her anymore. Whatever he'd felt that night had clearly dissipated in the two months since. She'd do what she came here for—work here long enough to get to know him, for the baby's sake. And find some way of telling him about their child. Then go back to San Diego.

Nothing more.

She wouldn't make the mistake of entangling herself again with a man who didn't share her visions of the future. Who would give her less than a hundred percent.

Linc raised a hand, and in an instant a sleek black town car glided to a stop before them. The driver hopped out, came around and opened the door for them. Linc gestured for Molly to enter first, then he slid in behind her, settling on the seat close enough for her to feel the heat of his body, but not close enough to touch.

"Your own driver?" she said. "I'm impressed." Once again, the differences between the Linc she'd met that night and the real Linc became readily apparent. The man she'd seen in the bar—had any of him been real? Who was the Lincoln Curtis sitting across from her? This stiff upper-lipped, wealthy, powerful CEO, not the average Joe she thought she knew two months ago.

What had he seen in her that night? And why hadn't he told her the whole truth about his life when they'd met? Perhaps, she thought, he'd met too many people who heard the word *millionaire* and immediately saw dollar signs instead of Linc.

"Don't be impressed, really," he said. "The car and driver are a necessity. A time-saver."

"Because driving your own car takes so much more time?" she joked.

"Because I can work while Saul drives." Linc gestured toward a laptop set up on a small desk on the left-hand side of the car, beside a built-in phone and a small television screen.

The Linc in the bar had seemed so relaxed, so ordinary, and yet this Linc seemed the complete opposite. It was more than the suit and the chauffeured car. He carried himself differently. As if a world of responsibility lay on his shoulders.

As the car pulled away from the curb, she glanced back at the towering building of Curtis Systems and realized perhaps it did.

Had she read him wrong that night? Or had her memory grown fuzzy over the last two months?

No, it wasn't that. He had definitely acted differently that night. The question was why.

"I thought you had a meeting to go to," she said. "The receptionist mentioned you were tied up all afternoon. Seriously, I don't mind coming back at a better time."

"I do have a meeting. I am swamped today." He let out a long breath, one that spoke of all those responsibilities. Then he looked over at her, as if he still couldn't believe she'd shown up on his doorstep. "But it's not every day that I receive…an unexpected visitor."

"That's a unique way of phrasing—" she was going to say *our relationship*, but they didn't really have one, so she settled instead on, "the situation."

"You caught me off guard today. I hadn't expected to see you again."

She caught the woodsy undertones of his cologne. In an instant she had an image of him from that night—simple pin-striped button-down shirt open at the collar, sleeves rolled up. But more than the way he'd dressed, she remembered the way he'd kissed, a kiss that had set her on fire in a way she never had been before. He'd taken his time, his lips drifting slowly over hers, his hand cupping her jaw, as if he was—

"How did you find me?" Linc asked.

"It, ah…" Molly drew her attention back to the present, her face hot "…wasn't that hard. There aren't that many software companies in Vegas employing a man named Linc, at least according to Google. I didn't know, however, that you *owned* Curtis Systems. I thought…" Her voice trailed off.

"Thought I was just a worker bee." A smile crossed his lips and he opened his mouth as if he was going to say something else, but his phone rang, cutting off the sentence midstream. Linc let out a sigh, checked the caller ID, then apologized to

Molly before answering the call. She heard him debating something about an architectural design for several minutes before he ended the call. Almost as soon as he hung up, his phone started in again. Linc sighed, then glanced at Molly. "Do you mind if I tie up a few loose ends before we go to lunch? This will only take a minute, I promise."

"Not at all. I understand."

He answered the first call, then placed several others, most of which Molly could tell from her one-sided interpretation were about cancelling the next few scheduled meetings and delegating responsibilities to other people within the company.

Linc didn't waste a single second. He powered up the laptop, working both that and the cell at the same time, in record time. She heard him run down several task lists, make at least a dozen different decisions, review several accounting issues with his comptroller, and all without becoming stressed or overwhelmed. If anything, Linc seemed to thrive on the stress of his job, as if heaping more things on his plate made it easier for him to carry.

What a stark contrast between her simple world of five-year-olds learning colors and numbers and Linc's of multi-million-dollar deals and corporate wrangling. Finally, he hung up, and closed the laptop. "Sorry about that."

"A CEO's job is never done and all that?" she said.

"Something like that." Linc tucked the phone into the holster on his belt. At the same time, the town car slid to a stop in front of an Italian restaurant with a bright red awning and several outdoor bistro-style tables. Linc stepped out of the automobile and offered a hand to Molly.

When her hand slipped into his large, familiar grip, that same electric jolt she remembered ran through her. Almost as quickly as he touched her, he released her.

Because he'd felt the same thing? Or because he was only being polite?

Molly decided not to ask. She had her priorities—to gain a job, as well as information for the baby. Besides, hadn't she learned her lessons with Doug? Long-term relationships and her didn't go together well. The last thing she needed was involvement with yet another man who didn't share her vision for the future, and already she would wager a guess that workaholic high-powered exec Lincoln Curtis wasn't looking to settle down in a little bungalow in San Diego with a kindergarten teacher and a baby.

She refused to feel disappointed. She hadn't come here with some happily-ever-after in mind. She and the baby would be just fine on their own, regardless of whether Lincoln Curtis ever wanted anything to do with her in the future.

A minute later, they were seated at a private booth in the back of the restaurant. "Would you like some wine?" Linc asked.

"Uh...no, thank you. I'll just stick to water." She shifted in her seat. "It's early yet."

"You're right." He didn't say anything more about the wine, and she was sure he hadn't guessed her real reason for turning down the alcohol. Warm garlic bread-sticks arrived with the water, then the waiter disappeared, leaving them alone.

Molly willed her queasiness to subside, and it did—just a little—with the bread. But still, she wasn't so sure she'd be able to eat.

"So...why now?" Linc asked. "Why come see me today, after two months?"

A flush invaded her cheeks. Did he know? Did the pregnancy show on her face? Had someone told him?

She shook off the thoughts. She was just being paranoid. Linc's question was legitimate, expected even.

She could tell the truth. She could tell him that she had thought about his eyes, his touch, a hundred, a thousand times since that night, but that would entangle the two of them together all over again, and Molly was far from ready for, or interested in, that. Especially when the feeling didn't seem to be reciprocated.

"I didn't come here to resurrect anything," she said, deciding the best course of action was to lay everything straight. Immediately. Before anyone got the wrong idea, or the train got derailed any further. "I came here because I was interested in that software program you mentioned."

Linc leaned back and draped an arm over the back of the booth. "I can't believe you remembered that."

"I thought it sounded so interesting. Interactive, inspires reading, while also teaching children about the great outdoors. Something that combines electronic learning and spurs interest in nature activities at the same time."

That had been one of their first conversations, and part of what had perked her interest in Linc. They'd started out talking birthdays, which had led into her job, then into how frustrated she was with kids being so sedentary and not tuned in with their environment, which had segued into Linc's software idea. Before she'd known it, she'd been wrapped up in his eyes, his voice, then his touch.

He'd been so excited about the software design, as if it was something personal. She'd enjoyed listening to him talk, and found his enthusiasm wrapping around her, too.

"That software…it was just an idea," Linc said. "My company doesn't really handle that kind of thing. We specialize in security packages for large corporations. Fraud prevention, hacker prevention, that kind of thing. The other program…that was a dream."

"Sounded like you were pretty serious that night."

"I…" He paused. "A long time ago, I used to think that was the kind of company I wanted to run. The kind of software I wanted to manufacture. But that's not where the money is, and when you run a business you have to be practical. In fact, I ran the idea past my team recently, and they shot it down."

Shot it down? He wasn't going to do it?

She'd come all the way to Vegas with an insane plan. Clearly, she hadn't thought it through enough. Or she'd completely misinterpreted what he'd said that night. She'd thought Linc had been serious about developing this software, and thus thought she would be the perfect one to help him implement the program, while at the same time getting to know her baby's father.

She'd invested everything in this one option—with no backup plan. That alone was proof she still wasn't thinking straight when it came to Lincoln Curtis.

It had to be the pregnancy hormones. Otherwise, why was she making such hasty choices?

"You have no plans to develop the program?" she said.

"I'd love to…someday." His gaze went to some far-off place, and he didn't say anything for a second, before he returned his gaze to her. "Why?"

Someday? She needed someday to be now.

She buried her attention in the menu. "No reason." Then she gave up studying the list of pastas and insalatas. "It's just…you sounded so excited when you talked about that program. It was as if *that* was the company you owned, not this one. In fact, that's what I thought when I met you.

When I arrived in Vegas, I was surprised to find out you made security systems."

He sighed, and pushed his menu to the side. "A long time ago—"

He didn't finish.

"A long time ago, what?"

The waiter returned and took their orders. Molly had barely looked at the menu, and just ordered one of the specials. Linc, who had clearly been here before, ordered a chicken and pasta dish.

"You started to say something before we were interrupted," Molly said, once they were alone again. "What was it?"

Linc took the green paper wrapper off his napkin and folded it into a triangle, then popped the triangle out. "Know what this is?"

She laughed. "No."

"To a kid, it's a boat. A hat. A Christmas tree. The possibilities are endless." He tipped the green cone onto the top of the salt shaker. It teetered, then balanced. "When I was a kid, I used to be like that. Everything I saw, I imagined into something else. My parents complained that I was always in my head, and never out in the world."

"I bet you read a lot."

He chuckled. "Everything I could get my hands on. I was a total bookworm. Still am."

"Me too." She grinned. "I love books."

A smile whispered between them. "Something we have in common, then?"

"I'd say so." Oh, she could feel that thread, that tenuous tether connecting them, just as it had that night. She tried to push it aside, to ignore the feeling. She didn't want to build a bridge. Not between herself and Linc. She was here for the baby. Only. "Go on with what you were saying."

"Well, my parents got tired of seeing me with my nose buried in a book twenty-four hours a day, so they shipped me off to a summer camp. One of those long, eight-week ones. My brother was there, too, but he was always the outdoorsy one. He took to camp like a duck to water."

"And you didn't?"

Linc snorted. "God, no. Took me seven of the eight weeks to fit in. But then one day a counselor noticed me reading instead of joining the other kids. He got me involved in a project, a camp diary thing. Creating a kind of written and photographed collage about camp that could be left behind for other campers. Sort of an intro to the best parts of camp."

His eyes lit up with the memory, his features became more animated. "You must have loved it."

He took a sip of his drink, then nodded. "I did. It was a brilliant idea on the counselor's part. A way to force me to go outside, collecting information and finding out about camp, in order to get back to my first love—books. In the course of doing that, I found out I loved being outside."

"And is that where the idea for the software came from?"

"Pretty much. My brother…he was the more adventurous one. Never met a challenge he didn't want to tackle. He loved the book. For him, it was a way to go back to camp over and over again, and…" Linc's voice trailed off and he paused for a long second. Then he cleared his throat and continued. "Anyway, he was the one who had the idea of taking the book and combining it with a computer program. Back in those days, of course, games and software were a long way from what they are now, and we were just kids, so we didn't know what we were doing. That first idea spurred the bug for the two of us later working together, forming the company, and our first project was always going to be that software, but…" He toyed with the green paper hat on the top of his straw.

"What happened?"

"The market research I did said the money wasn't in software for children. It was in security software. So we went with the better financial decision." He plucked the green triangle off the straw and crumpled it.

A practical man. She should be happy—it was, after all, the kind of commonsense decision that spoke to Molly's own practical nature. Instead, disappointment settled in her gut. What had she expected? The same wild spontaneity she'd seen in Linc that one night?

"Have you ever regretted that decision?"

"No. I did what was smart for the company. For the people who invested in it. The people who…believed in it from the beginning."

Even though he spoke with conviction, she detected a note of regret in his voice, the echoes of lost chances. "Now that you have the company to mega status—" at that, she smiled "—surely you have time to indulge a few of those earlier dreams. I mean, you are the boss. You and your brother could start building birdhouses and hula hoops if you wanted. Who's going to stop you?"

His face tightened. "I don't make decisions like that."

"Spontaneous ones, you mean?" Molly arched a brow.

His gaze met hers, and in that moment the two of them connected again, with a shared thought.

That night.

That amazing, spontaneous, heated, *insane* night.

"Well, I don't *usually* make spontaneous decisions," Linc said, and fire lit his blue eyes for just a moment before subsiding. "In business, every decision is based on research, numbers, financial projections."

"Where's the fun in that?"

He considered her words. "There is no fun in that. But it's reality. As you saw in the car, I'm an extremely busy man, which explains why my entire life revolves around work. Except for that one night, I pretty much live at the office, making all those non-fun decisions."

If anything screamed "not looking to be a family man," that did.

"So, it's not a matter of not wanting to create that software," Linc went on. "It's just about smart business practices. As my team pointed out, this has the potential to be a waste of company resources."

Clearly, his mind was made up. She would have to find another way to provide for her baby. And as for getting to know the baby's father—

She would simply tell Linc before she left town that she was pregnant and let him decide if he wanted to be part of the child's life or not. Maybe he would…or maybe he wouldn't.

The thought that he would turn his back on her and their child sent a wave of disappointment crashing over her. Regardless of how many times she told herself she hadn't expected an enthusiastic reaction to her presence—

She had.

She wanted to retreat, go home and lick her wounds. She'd been wrong, so, so wrong, and she needed to regroup, find another way of dealing with the mountain of worries in her chest. What was she going to do? How could she handle this on her own? Without a job, a father for her baby, a plan?

She grabbed her purse and started to slide out of the booth. "I'm sorry I took so much of your time. I thought when I met you that night…" She let out a breath. "I thought you were someone else, I guess." She rose and took a step, but Linc stopped her with a hand on her arm.

"Wait. Don't go," he said.

She hesitated, but didn't turn around. Beneath his palm, her nerve-endings pinged with awareness.

"Why are you really here, Molly?"

It was the way he said her name, in that same soft, husky way he'd said it that first night, that finally made her yield and turn back. "I told you. To ask about that job."

"I thought you were a kindergarten teacher."

"My position was cut for the coming school year."

"So that's why you decided to see me?" Linc said. "We only talked about that program for a little while before we…" A smile spread across his face. "Before we moved on to other things."

Oh, and they had moved on. And not returned from the kissing and touching for several hours. There'd barely been any words passing between them.

She pushed those thoughts aside. She wasn't here to relive that night in the Bellagio. Even if her mind kept straying in that direction every time she looked into Linc's blue eyes, or heard his voice or felt his touch. Nope, not going back there. No way.

Stick to the plan, Molly. Be smart. Not foolish again.

Molly returned to the booth, perching on the edge of the seat. "When you told me about that software, I saw a man who was alive, excited. That passion extended into your idea. I wanted to be on board with something like that. Not to mention be a part of developing a program that encourages kids to get outdoors and interact with nature, rather than stay inside, being couch potatoes and playing yet another video game."

His gaze connected with hers across the table. "You saw passion in me for this? A different person than you see today?"

She nodded.

He looked away for a moment, not at anything in particular, but out into the restaurant. She couldn't read whatever parade of thoughts was running through his mind. But when he turned back to her, the twinkle that had been in his blue eyes the night she'd met him had returned, and a funny quiver stirred in Molly's gut. "If we did this…and this is a big if…it would require a team of people to implement. Particularly people who know a lot about children."

She bit her lip. Dared to hope. "Like former kindergarten teachers?"

He smiled. "Exactly like former kindergarten teachers."

Molly took a deep breath and voiced the idea she'd had when she'd boarded the plane to Vegas and taken the biggest risk of her life—no, the second biggest risk of her life. "That's exactly why I came here, Linc. To offer you my services."

CHAPTER THREE

MOLLY HUNTER...working for him?

It was an insane idea, Linc thought, as the two of them delved into their food and he had a moment to think through what she had said and bring some rational perspective to an irrational idea.

After all, they'd only shared one night together—one incredible, amazing night. A night they'd both agreed not to take any further, to leave firmly in the past.

When he'd woken up the next morning with her in his arms, he had considered—for just a moment—taking this to the next step. Asking her to stay another day, a week, a month, to see him again. He'd been intrigued by the sweet and sassy kindergarten teacher who had seemed as ready as him to shed her ordinary life for something unforgettable, for just a few hours.

Then his phone had rung, and he'd been drawn back to reality. To a world that expected Lincoln Curtis to be responsible. The only logical choice had been the one that had seemed to leave Molly relieved and him back in his comfort zone of no personal relationships.

Hadn't he learned with Barbara that settling down wasn't for him? That he was the last man on earth who should be married? And if there was one thing he'd observed about Molly the more time he spent with her, it was that despite their crazy night she was a settling down kind of woman.

So they'd decided in the light of morning to go their separate ways, as if the night never happened. It would just be a great memory, they'd agreed. Since then, he'd been happy with that decision. Yes, he'd thought of her. What man wouldn't, with that long tousled mane of brown hair and those wide green eyes? But he'd left those thoughts in his memory. Not acted on them.

Did Molly have some hidden agenda for being here? Something she wasn't telling him? He sensed she was holding something back, but didn't know if it had anything to do with her wanting to work for him.

He watched her sip her drink, and in her heart-shaped face he saw only earnestness and honesty. Someone who was truly interested in his idea, the same one his best advisors had shot down as impractical.

All these years, he'd kept that idea on the back burner, saving it for some elusive "someday" in the future. The one promise he'd left unfulfilled, thinking he'd find a way to get to it, somehow. Now Molly sat before him, offering him the chance to bring that idea to life.

She'd called him "passionate" about the idea. Said she saw a man who was "alive, excited."

How long had it been since he would have used those adjectives to describe himself?

Yes, he went to work every day, doing a job he loved, but he had lost that charge, that zest, a long time ago.

No, not a long time ago. He could name the exact date his passion for this company had disappeared.

When he'd lost the one person who made coming into

work a memorable, fun experience. The person he had started the company with, built it with, the one that Linc had thought would always be there in the office beside his. From that day forward Linc had poured himself into the company, but being there had never been the same.

And here Molly Hunter came along, opening a door he hadn't even realized he'd shut.

Until now. Damn.

An odd thrill ran through him, a charge he hadn't felt in…forever. Since the first days when he'd started the company with Marcus, when every day had been an adventure, and they hadn't known if they were going to make a dollar or lose a dollar. For a man who kept his entire life on a tightly scheduled leash, the feeling was liberating. He recognized it—

From the night he'd met Molly.

It was a dangerous feeling. An addictive feeling. One he should put aside, as he had the morning after two months ago.

But as his gaze locked on Molly's emerald eyes, he found himself unable to let go of the idea he'd waited so long to bring to the table.

"You're really willing to uproot your life for this?" Linc asked her.

She nodded. "I'm at a point where I'm…" She paused. "Ready for big changes."

Was he?

Molly had certainly sprung a change on him when he'd least expected it. This woman, the one he'd thought he'd never see again, had suddenly popped up in his life—

With an offer to stay.

Albeit as an employee, not a girlfriend.

But wasn't that the perfect situation for him, really? For

all his talk this morning with Conner, what time did he have to start a relationship? He'd stepped away once, thought he could have it all—ditch the schedules and the memos in exchange for some fun and freedom. When he'd done that, Linc had broken the only promise he'd ever made—

To take care of his brother. And Marcus had paid with his life.

No, Linc, decided, now was not the time, no matter how tempting the thought of rekindling that night with Molly might be. Maybe once he took the company public, had placed a board of directors in charge...

And then where will you be? the little voice in his head asked. *Alone? Old?*

Better that than leaving a wife and two kids alone and grieving.

He was better off when his focus wasn't split, when the company remained his top priority. When his managers below him could have their lives and then come to work, happier and healthier. Someone had to be the captain, and that someone was Lincoln.

But...

Molly's idea offered him a taste of the dreams he'd once had. The ones he'd shared with his brother, then abandoned so many years ago. He wanted to do this. Wanted it badly—not for him, but for Marcus.

He thought of his schedule, of the relentless, dawn-to-dusk pace he kept, and couldn't see a way, as Conner had said, that he could fit this into his day, too.

Then a solution came to him. One that might give him the best of both worlds, allowing Linc to stay at the helm of the company while Molly did the work of overseeing the new software.

It wouldn't be the same as having a family of his own,

of course. But it would be something. A legacy, of sorts. One that he suspected he'd have more pride in than all the hacker prevention designs he'd perfected over the years.

It would be enough, Linc told himself. A fitting substitute for the one thing he had decided a long time ago he, of all people, would never have.

Yes, it would be enough.

Linc pushed his plate to the side. "I do have a preliminary program for this," he said to Molly. "Something that we worked up years ago..." He paused, his mind rocketing back to the time period he tried never to visit mentally. "If you'd be willing to work with me and my designers on it, give us the feedback we need for real-world applications, I think I could have something put together for launching next year."

She swallowed the bite of food in her mouth, considering. "How long do you think something like that would take? This working with the designers process?"

"At the very most, a few weeks. My team is pretty fast. And, like I said, the preliminary program is already there."

"Perfect. I just need something to tide me over until the next school year starts. I've put in several applications with other school systems, and I'm sure something will come through before September. I'm not looking for a career change, just a..." She put out her hands. "A bridge to my next job. If you're okay with that, then I think this will be a match made in heaven."

A flush filled her face. At the double meanings in the words? Or something else?

Once again, Linc was sure he detected an undercurrent of a hidden message, perhaps a secondary agenda, ever since she'd arrived. What it was, he couldn't discern. But it had him intrigued.

Could she still be interested in him? If so, he would have to make it clear that he had no intentions of starting a relationship, with her or any other woman. Regardless of how beautiful Molly was, or how memorable that night had been, his life was what it was. And that left no room for a woman like her.

A woman he had known, almost from the minute he met her, was the kind a man settled down with. Despite that one wild night. Molly Hunter, kindergarten teacher, had suburbia written all over her.

"I'm okay with that," Linc said. "Are you sure you are?"

"I wouldn't be here if I wasn't."

"I meant—" he leaned forward, his gaze connecting with hers, with the woman he had once spent an unforgettable, heated night with, one he had been unable to forget no matter how hard he tried and no matter what he told himself "—are you okay with working side by side with me for several weeks?"

What was more…was he?

Alex Lowell's squeal of joy could be heard from across the spacious, beautifully appointed lobby of McKendrick's Hotel. "Molly!" She drew her friend into a tight hug, the two months since they'd last seen each other disappearing in the space of the embrace. "I'm so happy to see you!"

Molly drew back, laughing. "I'm so happy to see you, too. San Diego just hasn't been the same without you and Serena. Even with all the texts, e-mails and video chats, it's not as wonderful as seeing my best friends in person."

Alex gestured toward a pair of love seats, and the two women took a seat. "I bet San Diego is a lot quieter," she said with a laugh of her own.

"Not quieter. More boring. Jayne and I still go to tea at

the tearoom, but we spend most of our time wondering how you two are doing." She grinned. "We had lots of great times at that place, the four of us."

The four of them had often gone to the Victorian Tea House, one of San Diego's favorite Old Town hangouts. They loved the food, the atmosphere, and most of all the opportunity for female bonding over cookies.

"We did have a lot of fun there," her friend agreed. "So, what brings you to Vegas? Besides seeing me and Serena, of course." Alex's sky-blue eyes danced with merriment.

Molly didn't think she'd ever seen her friend so happy. Glowing even. "Marriage agrees with you."

"Wyatt agrees with me," Alex said. "He's wonderful. I never thought I'd find a man so…" She paused and a smile spread across her face, the kind of smile Molly had read about in novels, imagined some women had for the men they loved, and once wondered if she would someday have on her own face. "So amazing. When he looks at me, I feel loved. He doesn't have to say a word. Just look at me."

A wave of envy ran through Molly, the force so strong it surprised her. She was happy with her life, glad she had gotten divorced. Doug had never once looked at her like that, and never, in fact, really taken the time to listen to her or understand her. And with a baby on the way, she had someone else's life to worry about—not her own.

Then why did she suddenly wish she could trade places with Alex? To have just a taste of the happiness emanating from Alex like sunshine?

Clearly, marrying Wyatt McKendrick, owner of McKendrick's, had been a good choice for Alex. Who would have thought when Alex had stayed behind after that wild weekend to work for Wyatt as his concierge, that she would have found love with the tall, dark-haired bachelor?

Now they were running the hotel together and obviously making their work and personal partnerships work.

"I'm so glad for you," Molly said, and meant it. "Really. You deserve all that and more."

"So do you," Alex said. "One bad marriage doesn't mean all of them are that way."

Molly didn't want to talk about her romantic life—or lack thereof—especially not after just leaving lunch with Linc, when everything inside her was still in turmoil after seeing him. Plus, being back in the lobby of McKendrick's, the very place where she and her friends had started their wild weekend two months ago, brought back every memory of meeting Linc and ending up in his arms, and later in his bed.

And she was hyper-aware of the results of that night. She felt every one of the changes in her body, even as minuscule as they were now. They all just kept reminding her that she was alone and pregnant, and though she now had a job, she had yet to find a way to tell Linc about the baby. A man who'd made it clear he wasn't interested in the hearth and home thing.

Molly sighed. "I don't have time for a relationship right now. I'm too busy starting a new job."

"A new job? What happened to teaching?"

"Cutbacks. So I'm taking a position here in Vegas until I can find another teaching job back in San Diego. It's a temporary thing, just a few weeks."

Alex blinked. Stared at Molly. "You're...you're uprooting your whole life for a temporary job in a strange city? You? Of all people?"

"What? It's not that unusual. People do it all the time."

"Yeah, *other* people. Not you." Alex reached out and laid a hand on Molly's arm. "You're the conservative one. The one who never does anything unpredictable or wild."

For a second, Molly wanted to tell Alex all about that night two months ago. To tell her good friend about how, for one moment, Molly had done something unpredictable and wild—

And ended up with very predictable, very serious consequences.

"You're right, Alex," Molly said instead. "Think of this as my first step into uncharted territory."

Except, was it the wisest step? When she'd left San Diego, she'd thought this was a brilliant plan. Now, after agreeing to work with Linc, second thoughts ran rampant in her mind.

Soon, she was going to have to tell him she was pregnant. And when he found out—

God, what if he wanted to marry her?

Then where would she be? Stuck in another bad marriage with a man who was her polar opposite, who'd proposed out of pity, or some outdated sense of honor?

No, thank you. She could handle this on her own. She'd just have to make that clear to Linc, right from the start.

Alex grinned. "Well, I don't care what the reason is for your trip here. I'm just happy to see you. I've missed you and Jayne so much! We'll have to get together for lunch, dinner, as much as we possibly have time for. And be sure to invite Serena, too. I know she's dying to see you as well."

Molly laughed. "I promise, we will. You have my cell number—give me a call anytime. Right now, I'm going over to the Hamilton Towers to get settled in and unpacked."

Alex arched a dark brow. "Hamilton Towers? Mighty fine digs for a temporary home."

"Linc is covering the costs as part of my salary." Molly felt her face heat. "I mean, Mr. Curtis."

"Linc?" Alex grinned. "First-name basis with the boss already?"

Goodness, the pregnancy must be making her forgetful. She hadn't told anyone about the man she'd met that night in the bar, and she wasn't ready to tell Alex now. "I...I met him before. A long time ago. And when he mentioned needing someone to head up this new educational software development program, I leaped at the chance to try something new."

A reasonable approximation of the truth. She wanted to tell Alex about the pregnancy, but just couldn't bring herself to explain it. Not yet. Not until she had completely come to terms with it herself.

And to do that, she had to come to terms with one other thing—

Lincoln Curtis.

CHAPTER FOUR

"You're crazy," Conner said to Linc the next morning. "But it's the kind of crazy I like."

Linc looked up from the stack of paperwork on his desk, a pile that seemed to have done nothing but grow since he'd arrived in the office a little after seven this morning. "What's that supposed to mean?"

"I heard about the new project." Conner dropped into one of the two visitors' chairs, his lanky frame dwarfing the antique mahogany seat. "So you're going forward with it after all?"

Linc nodded. "Call it an executive decision. I'm overriding the advice of all the other suits."

Conner chuckled. "It's about damned time."

Linc arched a brow. "What?"

"About damned time you did something that wasn't written into your schedule, something nobody expected you to do. My God, Linc, you've been living in a box way too long." Conner grinned. "I saw the gorgeous woman you hired to be in charge of the program, too. Don't try to tell me you don't have any ulterior motives involved here."

"I have—" Linc cut off the sentence. He refused to delve into his personal life with Conner. No matter how he tried to explain his and Molly's relationship, it was bound to come out wrong. There was just no way to start with "one-night stand" and end with "not interested in her" and come off believable. "I hired her to take the project off my hands. Nothing more."

A decision he'd cemented in his mind last night, after dropping Molly at Hamilton Towers, then asking Saul to make a circle of Vegas before returning to bring Linc back to the same building. He'd been too tempted to follow her into the building and to pick up where they'd left off two months ago. To invite her up to his penthouse apartment and see if the amazing chemistry they'd enjoyed before was still there.

It was the way she smiled at him, the way her green eyes seemed to dance with amusement, how those long, tempting locks of her dark brown hair curled gently around her face and shoulders. Everything about her seemed to beckon to him to take her back in his arms, to taste that sweet, silky skin again, to make love to her just one more time.

He'd left the restaurant wanting her more than he had when he'd first met her. They'd sat so close together in the town car—inches away from touching—and he'd been aware, so aware, of the floral notes of her perfume, the heat emanating from her body, the nearness of her silky skin. When she'd gotten out of the car, it had taken all his willpower to remain behind, giving her some excuse about needing to run an errand.

He'd had Saul drive until the urge passed—or at least had been conquered by his better sense—and then he took the express elevator straight to his apartment, ignoring the whisper of temptation to stop at the apartment he'd given her on the tenth floor.

"You *are* insane," Conner said. "If I was you and that woman was a few floors away, I'd—"

"You know how busy I am," Linc said, interrupting Conner before he gave voice to the very thoughts that had been plaguing Linc for hours. "For God's sake, we're right in the middle of designing the East Coast offices, we've got the product launch for next year's security suite coming up in the fall, and—"

"And if I let you, you'll find ten more reasons why you can't find time to go on a simple date. Did you pay any attention at all when that woman came by to talk to you yesterday? You would have to be dead, Linc, not to be attracted to her. What would it hurt to ask her out?" Conner leaned forward and put a hand on the papers on Linc's desk. "I'm not the boss, and I don't pretend to be, nor do I presume to know what's on your shoulders, Linc. But I do know that beautiful women don't come walking through the doors of this company every day, looking for a job that entails working side by side with *you*."

True. And for a second the thought of seeing Molly Hunter every day, of being beside her again, inhaling the intoxicating notes of her perfume, or hearing the lilting sound of her laugh, tempted him all over again. "I've already asked Roy to handle the project. He's got the expertise, the background—"

"But not the passion. Linc, this thing is your baby. You've been talking about it for years."

"I'll communicate with Roy," Linc said. "Aren't you the same person who told me my schedule didn't have enough room in it for one more thing?"

"That was before I saw you with Molly." Conner grinned. "You can talk all you want about not being interested in her, but I saw it in your face. You are."

Linc gave Conner a pointed look. "I have to get back to work."

Conner stepped back and put his hands up. "Suit your-self. But I think you're passing up a prime opportunity to have what everyone else has."

Linc's gaze had already dropped to the profit and loss statement before him. The numbers, however, were a blur. "And what's that?"

"A life." Then Conner walked out.

Linc let out a sigh and dove into the numbers and charts, telling himself that finding solace here would be the best decision all around. All he needed to do was take one look at the empty office next door if he needed a reminder of why he should stay behind this desk, instead of running off like some infatuated teenager. With the very woman who had made him forget his life for one very unforgettable night.

Work. Don't think about Molly. Be smart. Concentrate.

Linc lasted until ten.

Then he gave up the pretense of working—his concentration had been shot to hell pretty much from the minute his assistant had told him Molly had arrived—and headed down to the sixth floor.

He'd just check on the project. Nothing more. Then he could go back to work and focus.

When he reached the Research and Development room, he paused outside the open door. Molly was half-seated on one of the desks, looking over the shoulder of Roy, one of the company's graphic designers. Jerome, another graphic designer, sat at a companion computer, also working on the program. The two of them were typing away on the keyboard, inputting computer code at record speed.

Molly laughed at something Roy said, the sound as light and cheery as spring sunshine. Linc found himself smiling, and wanting to know what joke had coaxed such a nice sound from Molly.

At the same time an odd surge of something Linc refused to call jealousy rushed through him. He hadn't been the one to make her laugh, or to bring that smile to her lips.

"How's it going?"

Molly pivoted at the sound of his voice. "Linc."

His pulse kicked up as the single syllable of his name rolled off her tongue, with that soft lilt of surprise. This was trouble—bad trouble. He'd come down here merely to check on their progress. Stop in, ask a couple questions and leave.

And already he found his gaze searching the room for another chair. A free space beside Molly.

Roy turned toward Linc. "Going great, Mr. Curtis," he said. "We're making good progress. Since you already had the preliminary design worked out, Molly is helping us come up with different modules within the software. I should have a working model within a few days. Nothing finished, mind you, but a rough idea for you to see."

Linc nodded. Roy turned back to the computer, and to Molly. Linc knew that was his cue—he was free to go. He'd gotten what he came for, a status report.

Molly waved him over. "Do you want to come see?"

That was all it took. The steps he'd been about to take out the door became steps across the room to her side. He gestured toward the notebook beside her. "I take it you were able to understand my notes?"

Molly laughed. "I can read kindergarten writing, which is…creative, to say the least, when they're learning to make letters. I can read yours."

He grinned at her. "You're comparing me to a kinder-gartener?"

She returned his smile and something he thought he'd been able to bury in the two months since he'd met her was resurrected. "If the handwriting fits."

Roy cleared his throat. "Hey, Jerome. I think it's about time for a coffee break, don't you?"

Jerome grunted, and kept on working. Roy leaned over and smacked him on the shoulder. "Jerome, dude. Coffee."

Jerome looked up. Looked at Roy, then his eyes widened, and he looked at Linc, then Molly. "Oh. Coffee. Yeah. I could really use a cup."

The two men couldn't have been more obvious if they'd hung up a billboard. They hurried out of the room, leaving Linc and Molly alone.

Molly had her attention buried in Linc's notes, so she barely noticed the departure of the other men. She was still sitting on the edge of the desk, which made her floral print A-line skirt hike up just above her knees. She wore low heels and a short-sleeved pink shirt with a scooped neck. Conservative, but to Linc, who knew that underneath the elementary school teacher lurked a wild side, the outfit had the added edge of seeming to tease and tempt.

He shook his head. Thinking of that night wouldn't do him any good. At all. "So," he said, forcing himself to focus on the computer screen, "what direction were you thinking of going in?"

She put the notebook aside. "Well, I know my students really like exploration activities. Things that make them search for something, then learn about it. So we were thinking of having a find-the-animals game, sort of like the classic memory game, here." She pointed at the screen, where some rudimentary icons had been placed on the home page. "And then, when they unearth, say, the koala bears in the trees, they get to move on to the next level, which is an interactive learn-about-koalas game."

Linc nodded. "Great idea. A reward for winning the first game, one that encourages even more learning."

"Yep. Sort of like getting ice cream for finding the cookie jar. Which is definitely my idea of a reward."

He laughed. "I like that. We should use it in the marketing materials." He slid into the chair beside her, and as he did he caught the scent of her perfume, sending his mind spiraling back to the memory of kissing her neck, tasting her skin.

Not doing such a good job of focusing there, Linc.

She shifted toward him, and the minuscule closing of the gap only increased his awareness of Molly. "Tell me more about what you envisioned with this program," she said.

He tried to come up with an answer to her question, and had trouble envisioning anything that didn't involve her and the bed at the Bellagio.

"Linc?"

Focus on business. Numbers.

"Uh, software that will capture a significant portion of the four-to-seven-year-old market share," he said, "as well as the elementary school market. Something that will combine children's natural curiosity tendencies with—"

"I meant something personal."

He paused. "Personal?"

She nodded, then leaned in closer to him. Inquisitive. Probing. "Tell me more about your camping experiences. About why this is so special to you. Those are the kinds of things I really want to be sure to include."

Get involved, she was saying. Put aside everything else and be a part of this. With her. In other words, stop spending so much time in the tightly scheduled world he had known for so long, among the comfort of his task lists and memos.

That was exactly the area he was trying to avoid. A place he hadn't gone in such a long time. Not since his relationship with Barbara. Then, he'd thought opening his heart, getting close to someone, would be a good choice.

Only to find out that he was wrong. If anyone wasn't cut out for traditional, it was him.

If Molly had asked him a question about marketing projections, profit potential, advertising expenditures, the answer would have been no problem. But delving into the personal meant dancing around the edge of a relationship.

"This doesn't have to be about camping, Molly. It can be about anything outdoorsy. Bugs, trees, rocks." Linc waved a hand. "Whatever interests that age group. The goal with the software, as you know from our first conversation, is to encourage the kids to take what they learn and apply it in the real world. To get them off the couch and outside. That's what you're here for, to find out what will do that. You're my expert in that arena. And you have my notes—that should be enough."

"But this is *your* project, Linc. To make it work, I…" She stopped, started again. "The team needs your input." She picked up the notebook and flipped a few pages. "For example, in here you were talking about a game you and your brother used to play. I thought it sounded really fun, and something we could convert to the software. What was it called?" She ran her finger down the page. "Something with an animal name—"

"Water Snakes." The memory slammed into him, hard and fast. Marcus and him in the backyard, one of them holding a hose, while the other tried to outrun the spray. Sometimes they'd get a bunch of the neighborhood boys involved, and before the day was done the game had turned into a slippery, laughing mess on the lawn.

The last time he'd played that game he'd been in Marcus's backyard. With his brother, and his brother's two children. He could still hear Anna's and Daniel's laughs, still see the surprise on their faces when the water splashed their legs.

A week later, there had been nothing for the children to laugh over.

Because of Linc.

"Yes, that's it," Molly said. "I think we could use something like that in the software. Make it a techno-dodgeball kind of thing. I wanted to learn more about how the rules worked, so I could—"

"I don't have time for this right now," Linc said. "I have work to do."

"I don't need you to spend hours here, Linc." She smiled. "I just want to pick your brain for a little while."

The room suddenly felt close, hot. He pushed back the chair and rose. "I should probably leave you to this. Really, you know this age group better than I do. I have a meeting to get to."

A meeting Connor could handle as easily as he could. A meeting he could miss with a simple phone call. A meeting he wanted to miss—just to see Molly smile at him again.

But she kept pushing the very buttons he had marked Off-Limits.

And for good reason.

Molly slid off the desk and the distance between them went from feet to mere inches. "I'm not letting you off that easily."

He arched a brow. "You're…what?"

"You hired me to head up this project. And as the head of this project, I'm—" she took in a breath and drew herself up "—well, I'm ordering you to be a part of it."

What was she doing? Couldn't she see he wanted to leave? Her take-charge attitude surprised him, set him off kilter. He was used to being the boss—not having anyone boss him back. Oh, this woman was trouble. So much trouble.

"I'm the CEO, Molly, you can't do that. I sign your checks."

She grinned. "And I can't move forward without the input of the creator." She put out her hands. "Seems we're at an impasse, Mr. Curtis."

The formal use of his name sent a charge through him. Thousands of people called him that on a regular basis, but when he heard it from Molly's lips his name sounded like a flirtation.

Leave, his common sense told him. *Go back to work. You have no business getting close to a woman like her.*

A woman who deserves…what you can't and shouldn't give.

He rose and took a step closer to her, ignoring the warning bells sounding in his head. Seeing only her eyes, her smile, her lips. "It does, doesn't it?"

She inhaled, surprise lighting in her eyes as he closed the gap between them. "Then whatever shall we do?"

He knew what he wanted to do. He wanted to continue what they had started two months ago. He wanted to kiss her again, to take her home to his apartment, and to take days, not a single night, to explore every inch of her sweet skin.

To kiss her from head to toe. To make love to her again and again, until the ache he felt every time she was near finally went away.

The ache, the need, for the impossible. For what his brother had had. For that window of the happily-ever-after.

He reached up a hand, capturing one long, brown lock in his grasp. It slid through his fingers like silk, and the memory of her in his arms rocketed through him. Her lips parted, and the urge to kiss her, to taste her lips again, pounded in his brain.

God, he wanted her. He'd always wanted her. That wasn't the problem.

Having her was.

His cell phone vibrated against his hip, and reality intruded. He had people waiting for him. What the hell was he doing? He needed to be smart, sensible. Not irrational. Not let his hormones control his judgment.

Linc stepped back, breaking the contact. "I'm sorry, but my time is too limited to be much help to you. Roy knows me well enough," he said. "That's why I made him chief graphic designer on this project. I'm sure with his help you'll be able to develop this without further input on my end."

Then he turned on his heel and left, before being responsible became synonymous with being miserable.

At the end of the day, Molly journeyed up in the company elevator, telling herself she should be leaving. Going back to Hamilton Towers. Her work was done for the day—everyone else in the building had gone home—

Everyone except for Linc.

She'd known that because she'd gotten an e-mail from him five minutes ago. Direct, to the point, never veering from the topic of business. If she was smart, she'd take it as what it was—a clear sign that he wanted nothing more than work between them.

Except…

She'd seen something in his eyes today. Something that brought her back to that night they'd spent together.

Not to mention there was a lot more between them than that. Her hand strayed to her abdomen. She needed to tell him about her pregnancy, somehow. Maybe if she caught Linc alone, she'd find a way.

The elevator doors opened on the floor for the corporate offices and Molly stepped into the silent hall. Only a few lights burned, and it gave the entire space an all too intimate feel. Reminded her it was only she and Linc on this floor, maybe a few security people scattered throughout the building. For all intents and purposes, though, they were alone.

Last time they'd been alone in a darkened space, they'd ended up in bed together. Well. That wouldn't happen this time, Molly vowed. She turned to the right, headed down the hall, then rounded the corner.

And nearly collided with Linc.

Surprise lit his blue eyes. "Molly. You're still here?"

"Working late. Like you." She smiled.

"Did you get a lot accomplished today?"

She nodded. "Roy and Jerome are really talented. They blew me away, the way they could take the ideas I had and turn them into a reality with just a few clicks of the mouse. Oh, and we came up with a name, too. We were thinking of calling it Inside Out Games."

He nodded. "I like that."

A thrill ran through her. "Good."

Oh, that was bad. She shouldn't be so happy that Linc was pleased with the name of the computer game, for goodness' sake. She should instead be focusing on her goal—getting to know Linc and finding a way to tell him about the results of their night together.

Results…like thinking about the baby growing inside of her with such a detached word could take one bit of the emotion out of it for her. Every time she thought of the pregnancy, she was thrown into an emotional tailspin of what-ifs and what-will-I-dos.

"Tomorrow, when you start on the module for—"

"I don't want to talk about work," she cut in. "I need to ask you something."

He shifted his stance. "Shoot."

Before she could change her mind, she blurted out the question that had plagued her for weeks. "Why just one night?" One day, that would be a question her son or daughter would ask. Why had they only spent that single night together? Why hadn't Linc wanted more? Wanted something more permanent? "I mean, I don't know about you, but I am not a one-night-stand kind of person. At all. That night was such a total—"

"Aberration."

"Yes. Exactly."

He took a step closer. "For me, too." His gaze searched hers, and she wondered what he read there, or, more precisely, what he was looking for. "But I don't do commitments or relationships well, Molly."

"Because?"

He let out a breath. "Another complicated question."

He wasn't making this easy. Nor was he exactly an open book. What had she expected, really? That she would step off the elevator and Lincoln Curtis would just plop his heart on the table for her to examine?

Her stomach began to rumble, then churn. She'd skipped lunch because she hadn't felt well, and had meant to grab some crackers out of the breakroom, but got so busy she forgot. Now the morning sickness, which was a total misnomer considering it was almost seven at night, had returned with a vengeance.

"I was serious today," she said, trying to ignore the growing upset in her abdomen, "about wanting to get to know you better."

A smile curved across his face. "You are one determined woman."

"Not ordinarily. I'm just..." She searched for the words, the explanation for this new Molly, this woman who was trying to grab the reins because there was suddenly more at stake.

"Just what?" Linc asked when she didn't finish.

Her stomach pitched and rolled. God. She was going to be sick. She had to get out of here.

"Molly? Are you all right? You look a little pale."

"I'm—" she took a breath "—fine. Really."

This was *not* the way she wanted to tell him about the baby—just as she dashed off to the ladies' room.

Linc reached for her, his face filled with concern, but before his touch could connect with Molly she mumbled an excuse about being late—

And hurried down the hall, escaping just before she announced her pregnancy in the worst possible way.

CHAPTER FIVE

MOLLY picked at her dinner, pushing the chicken from one side of the plate to the other, piling the risotto into a mountain that she knocked down again with her fork. She was sitting in Sparkle, the beautiful, plant-draped, sun-kissed rooftop restaurant at McKendrick's with Alex and Serena Benjamin, who had begged off from attending a political fundraiser with her new husband, Jonas, to come to dinner instead. Molly knew she should be excited to be reunited in person with another of her best friends, but she couldn't seem to find the energy.

"What gives, Molly?" Alex asked. "You're not exactly the life of the party tonight."

"Are you feeling okay?" Serena asked, concern filling her green eyes. "You've hardly eaten a bite."

Molly put down her fork and pushed her plate to the side. "No. Yes." She sighed. "Maybe."

Alex and Serena laughed and exchanged a glance.

"No. Yes. Maybe," Alex repeated. "That's like saying everything all at once. What are you, sick?"

"No. Yes." Molly let out a breath. "I mean, I'm fine, I'm not sick, but—"

"That has to be the weirdest answer ever," Serena

agreed. "The only time I know of when a woman feels awful but is totally cool with it is when she's pregnant and there's no way…" Serena stopped talking. Stared at Molly.

Molly swallowed hard. A weak smile wobbled on her lips. She put out her hands and shrugged.

"Molly?" Alex said.

"You're not. Are you?"

Molly nodded. "I just found out."

Alex and Serena both exploded in cries of joy, drawing Molly into twin hugs so fierce Molly nearly couldn't breathe.

"Two months?" Alex said. "I can't believe you didn't tell us. How did this happen? I mean…" Then the light-bulb went on. Her jaw dropped, her eyes widened. "Two months ago we were here. In Vegas."

Molly nodded again. She had to tell them. These women were two of her best friends. Eventually she would start showing, and the questions would start. She had to come up with answers. How could she possibly tell people—strangers, casual friends, oh, God, her *mother*—that this pregnancy was the result of a one-night stand? But with her best friends, she could—and should—tell the truth. After all, they'd been there, and they, of all people, would understand.

Molly took a deep breath, then plunged forward with the story. "Remember the second night we were here, how we all kind of went our separate ways?"

Serena nodded. "You and I went to one of the bars at the Bellagio, but then you said you had a headache and you were going back to our room."

"I did. And I was. But as I was leaving I stopped in another lounge, this wonderful piano bar, thinking maybe a glass of wine would help me feel better." Heat filled Molly's cheeks. "And while I was sitting there, I met someone."

She could see it all over again, as if she were in the Bellagio's Baccarat Bar right now, the lights dim, the pianist playing jazz music softly in the background. And then, when she'd been about to leave, Linc had taken the seat beside her, and changed everything. "He slipped onto the stool next to me and ordered a bourbon on the rocks. He was handsome—really handsome—but that wasn't what intrigued me."

"What?" Serena leaned forward, her green eyes wide beneath a fringe of auburn hair.

"It was his eyes," Molly said. "When I looked at him, he looked…" She searched for the right word to describe the Linc she had met that night, the one word that could capture the reason she had decided to flirt with him, and later, sleep with him. "Lost."

Alex had pushed her dinner aside, too, the three of them engrossed in the conversation instead of the meal. "Lost as in needing a GPS system or some other kind of lost?"

"Like he was searching for who he was." And oh, how she could relate to him. To the year she had spent married, thinking she'd made the biggest mistake of her life, then the two years after the divorce, looking for her footing again. That was what she had felt, too. Lost, trying to find out who she was and what she really wanted in life. She thought she'd known—until the last couple of months. "So I started talking to him."

"You started talking to him?" Alex repeated. "You? The woman who gave us a stern lecture about *not* talking to strangers the whole way down here?"

Molly laughed. "Maybe it was the alcohol. Maybe it was being in Vegas. Maybe it was seeing what happened to Jayne when her engagement broke up so disastrously and I just sort of had this *carpe diem* moment, but, yes, I introduced myself, and mentioned that I was a kinder-garten teacher in town with friends for the weekend."

"How did you go from that to…?" Serena gestured toward Molly's belly.

"We found out we had a lot in common." Or at least, she'd thought that at the time. The man she had met that night had been so much more relaxed, looser. Happier. Not so buttoned-down and scheduled. Had it been the alcohol? The setting? Or something else? Something real? "And there was an attraction there. A really big one."

She could still feel the desire that had sizzled between them. The breathless anticipation that had caught in her throat after the first time they'd kissed and she'd wondered when he would kiss her again, touch her again. Her mind painted a crystal clear picture, as if she was there now and Linc was a breath away from touching her.

"And you decided to act on that attraction with a perfect stranger?" Alex said, interrupting Molly's thoughts. "That is so out of character for you, Molly."

"I know. Which I guess is why I did it. One minute I'm talking to him, the next we're holding hands, then kissing, and before we know it we're getting a room upstairs. I wanted to…" She let out a long breath and looked past her friends, down the Vegas strip, not seeing the flashing neon and endless sea of twenty-four-hour businesses, but seeing instead the person she'd been for that one night. Someone other than dependable, predictable Molly, who did the same thing every single day, and hadn't seen anything good come out of it except a bad marriage and a worse divorce. "I wanted to see what it would be like if I acted on my impulses. Just once."

"And how was it?" Serena asked, a devilish grin cross-ing her lips. "Acting on your impulses, I mean."

Molly sighed. "Wonderful." Amazing. Incredible. There weren't enough adjectives in the thesaurus to describe that evening. The way he'd taken his time, made her feel like the only woman in the world. She'd felt treasured, special, beautiful. The night had been hot and passionate, yes, but at the same time oddly romantic.

"So…where is Mr. Wonderful? Does he know about the baby?"

"He's here, in Vegas." Completely not the same Mr. Wonderful as that night, but Molly didn't add that. If she did, she'd probably cry, and she refused to shed one tear over Linc. She had too much to look forward to right now with the baby. "And, no, he doesn't know. I'll tell him. Soon."

Alex sat back and eyed Molly. "I get the feeling you're leaving out part of the story. Maybe the most important part. Like what happened when you got to Vegas and reunited with super-hot guy from the bar."

"Nothing happened. When I saw him again, he wasn't… the same as when I met him before." She toyed with her drink. Her appetite had deserted her, replaced by the bitter taste of disenchantment. She'd pictured such a different scenario than what she'd gotten upon her arrival in Vegas. That's what she got for reading so much fiction. "I just need time to decide what to do."

"I understand that." Serena fiddled with the wedding ring she wore, and Molly wondered how things were going between Serena and Jonas. There'd been an obvious chemistry with the couple, but that didn't mean their marriage of mutual convenience was going to work out.

At the same time Molly had been with Linc, Serena had been marrying Jonas, a total stranger, in one of those chapels of love. She'd agreed to stay married to him, though, and help him in his run for mayor of Las Vegas, so maybe things weren't all bad. Although Serena didn't have that same happy glow as Alex.

Molly wanted to ask, and started to, but Serena's face brightened and she spoke before Molly could. "Well, I think having a baby is exciting, even if it's with Mr. Wrong. I know you'll figure out the right time to tell him, Molly. And maybe when you do it'll change everything." She reached over and drew Molly into a hug. "Either way, no matter what, a baby is a happy thing. A blessing. So I say we celebrate with some chocolate cake!"

They ordered three desserts and toasted the pregnancy, and for the first time since she'd seen those two pink lines Molly began to feel a swell of happy anticipation. That was the best part about having such good friends—they were there when she needed them, and they could help her see past the gray skies to the sunshine waiting on the other side.

Linc begged off early from the business dinner, pleading a headache, and had Saul drive him home. In reality, he'd been in no mood to conduct business since he'd walked out of the R & D room yesterday. Lord knew he'd done his best to concentrate, putting in extra hours, heaping more onto his "To Do" list, accepting every meeting request that came his way. But it hadn't helped.

Every time he looked at a spreadsheet, every time he answered an e-mail, every time he picked up his phone, he saw Molly's face, heard Molly's voice, caught the scent of Molly's perfume.

Last night, his dreams had centered around her. His mind had replayed that night they'd met, starting with the first time their hands had collided, skipping forward to when he'd leaned over and kissed her, and a surge of desire had rushed through him.

There'd been another kiss after that, a third, a fourth, each ratcheting up the heat level until it became pretty clear they were crossing the boundaries of what was acceptable in a public place. At the same time, they'd both said the words "get a room," and as fast as he could lay down his credit card they were in a suite at the Bellagio.

Not that they ever noticed the elegant décor. It had been a frenzy of kicking off shoes, shedding shirts, pants—their clothes leaving a Hansel and Gretel trail all the way to the bed. And only then, when he finally had Molly's sweet, silky body against his, did he pause to take the time to taste her skin, to shower her with kisses, to slow the tempo enough to enjoy the beautiful woman in his arms.

To make the night unforgettable.

Considering how vividly those moments still starred in his memory, that goal had definitely been accomplished on his end. Many times over.

Molly. He knew he shouldn't, but he wanted to see her again.

The town car slowed to a stop outside the Hamilton Towers building, right behind a taxi. Linc was home, as much home as a penthouse apartment in a city that never slept could be. Another night alone—one he'd probably spend going over reports, drinking a glass of bourbon, then falling asleep far too late before getting up far too early. Linc thanked Saul and got out of the car. At the same time the door of the taxi opened—

And Molly emerged, as if he'd conjured her up simply by thinking about her. She wore a knee-length black dress that outlined her every curve, and reignited the very desire he'd been trying so hard to ignore.

Ever since she'd arrived in Vegas, he'd tried to pretend he hadn't been affected at all by her reappearance in his life. When in truth, he'd been lying to himself. He'd been very much affected.

He just couldn't—and shouldn't—do anything about it. He'd made a promise, but damned if he could remember it whenever Molly was nearby.

She turned and saw him. "Hi, Linc."

"Seems we finished our dinners at the same time." He wanted to ask her where hers had been, but more, *who* she had had dinner with, but he couldn't find a way to do that without seeming like an overprotective father or jealous boyfriend. And he was neither.

Molly drew her wrap tighter around her shoulders. "Goodness, it's chilly in Vegas when the sun goes down."

"Here." He slipped off his suit jacket and swung it over her shoulders, allowing his hands to linger just a second.

"Thanks." She smiled up at him. "Much warmer now."

He was, too, but not because of what he was wearing— because he was never going to look at a suit jacket the same way again. Molly's curvy figure gave his tailored coat a whole new look. One he wasn't going to forget anytime soon.

Linc started walking beside her into the building. He held the door for Molly, brushing off the doorman's attempt to get it first. At the elevator, he pressed the button for up. He should let her go home, allow the evening to end without any further interaction. She was his employee now.

Nothing more.

And that was exactly what he wanted, what he'd been telling himself he needed. Except…

That yawning hole he'd felt two months ago had returned with a vengeance, and he found himself craving what Molly had to offer. Lightness, fun, an opportunity to be someone else for just a little while. To let go of the burdens he'd carried for so long.

What would it hurt, just tonight? One more night, he told himself. Just one.

Linc turned, putting his back to the elevator. "I have a crazy idea. Are you game for something…different tonight?"

A smile curved up one side of her face, the smile he remembered from when he'd first met her, and that craving roared even stronger in his gut.

"Something different?" She considered. "What are you proposing?"

"A little bit of Vegas not everyone sees. Something off the tourist track."

She hesitated a moment, her head cocked, studying him. "Okay. I'm game."

"Good." Once outside, Linc hailed a cab, since he'd already sent Saul home for the night. "Let's tour a little of the city first." He gave the driver some directions, then sat back beside Molly as they drove down the streets of the city.

Having lived in Vegas for most of his life, Linc had, of course, seen the city a thousand times at night. But he had never seen it through Molly's eyes. The sun had set, and as darkness gathered over the streets, the ubiquitous lights brimmed with life, reflecting off her face in a bright, happy rainbow.

"It's beautiful, isn't it?" she said as they drove.

"In its own way, yes."

"I mean, you expect it all to look tawdry, but the colors are gorgeous."

Like you, he wanted to say, but didn't.

"Stop here," he said to the driver. "And wait for us." He got out, took Molly's hand and led her down a wide street lined with busy casinos, shops and hotels, all housed under a giant canopy.

"This is amazing," Molly said. She stopped walking,

spinning a little to take it all in. Linc turned with her, allowing Molly's wonder to rub off on him. The emotion was as sweet as dessert, and as rarely indulged, at least in his life.

He had the strongest urge to kiss her, to take her in his arms again. Instead, he cleared his throat and started reciting every fact he could think of. "This is Fremont Street, one of the most famous landmarks in Vegas. The canopy covers about a quarter-mile tract. Above you are 12.5 million synchronized LED lights—"

Molly pressed a finger lightly against his lips. "I love the information, Linc, really, I do, but just for one minute let's enjoy it."

He opened his mouth to speak, nearly kissing her finger. Oh, that was trouble. "Uh…sure."

She smiled. "Enjoy it," she repeated.

They stopped and looked up at the kaleidoscope of animations and videos marching across the canopy, which changed every few minutes, zipping from images of space to shorts about alien battles. Linc found himself laughing with Molly—enjoying the frenetic, skyward show. After a while, they started wandering among the shops.

She held up a clock shaped like a giant pair of dice. "This, I think, is totally you, Linc."

He grinned. "Oh, yeah?"

"Absolutely." She turned it right, left, her face a mask of seriousness, but he could see her biting her lip to keep from bursting into laughter. "Exactly what today's CEO needs to stay on time."

A moment later they walked out of the shop, with one dice-shaped clock in tow. "Now we'll have to get you something suitably Vegas."

She grinned at him. "And what would that be?"

He faked as if he was reaching for a glow-in-the-dark

martini glass, and instead picked up a teddy bear embla-
zoned with the logo of a nearby hotel. "This." He danced
the bear in front of her, grinning. "It's warm, fuzzy and
available to cuddle. A perfect Vegas memento."

Molly knew Linc meant the item as a joke. That he
didn't see the hidden meaning in a small stuffed toy. But
still, the image of Linc bending over a crib, handing their
baby the same small white bear, sprang to her mind. She
turned away, afraid he'd be able to read her thoughts on her
face. "Oh, yeah, perfect."

"You don't like it?"

"No, no, of course I do." But the words rang false, no
matter how cheery a spin she put on them.

"Maybe you'd rather have some of these Elvis sunglasses?" Linc held up a pair of amber shades, and gave
her another smile. She said something that passed as a
joke and moved on to the next tacky souvenir.

She should have told him. She'd had an opening, a
moment she could have said something, but let it pass. Of
course, they were standing in the middle of a busy store, on
their first real "date," if she could even call it that. Probably
not the best time to drop the pregnancy bombshell.

They left the store and started heading back toward the
taxi. "You feeling okay?" Linc asked. "You look a little pale."

"I'm fine." But she wasn't.

"Do you want to see one more place? Something a little
different?"

"Sure." Anything to get out of here. Away from the
teddy bear and all that implied.

Lincoln Curtis should know better. He had, after all, tried
the relationship route once before. He'd come within
inches, in fact, of walking down the aisle. Even briefly

toyed with the idea of becoming a father, having the whole American dream of two-point-five kids and a house in the suburbs.

Then Marcus had died, his life had fallen apart, and he'd realized he was better off staying right where he was—behind a desk.

Except, every time he looked into Molly's deep green eyes, he forgot the reasons why he'd made those resolutions. He was rocketed back to that night in the bar, and a part of him—a part he thought he'd managed to bury—came to life and said he deserved a life, if only for a moment.

The part that forgot the legacy he had taken on, one he had managed so badly thus far. The promises he had made to his parents before they died. To his brother, then, after Marcus was gone, to his brother's family. One of these days, he vowed, he would get all of that right. Getting distracted by a relationship wasn't going to help.

That's what he told himself. Twice.

"Where are we?" Molly asked, as the cab pulled away.

"It's my friend Harry's place. He opened it a few years ago. It's not your typical Vegas tourist place, and I thought you might like it." Linc gestured toward the sign above the bright blue door, which Molly could read now that they were under the exterior lights.

Harry's Underwater Experience:
Guaranteed to Thrill and Amaze.

"Underwater Experience?" Molly asked. "We're not scuba diving, are we?"

Linc laughed. "No. It's not that adventurous. Just a lot of interesting fish. And an interesting owner."

"An aquarium?"

Linc shrugged. "Of sorts. Harry's got a unique sense of humor, and it shows here. I think you'll like it."

Molly smiled and marveled at Linc's choice of destination. Of all the places he could have named, this probably wouldn't have made the list. Once again, Lincoln Curtis had surprised her. Before Molly could ask him any more questions, Linc had led her inside the busy lobby, and drawn her over to the glassed-in ticket booth, which was framed by dozens of cartoon aquatic animals. "Harry, you have room for two more?"

The wizened old man behind the ticket counter looked up from counting change and gave Linc a wide grin. "Linc! Long time no see! I was beginning to think I'd never get you in here to see my new leopard sharks."

Linc laughed. "I'm a bit busy, Harry."

"Excuses, excuses."

"It's not an excuse, it's a job," Linc said, giving the older man a friendly grin. "Somebody's got to steer the ship."

"One of these days, you'll be my age, and you'll be wishing you took more time off when you were young." Harry shook his head. "Anyway, you're here now, and with a beautiful lady at that. Let's enjoy the night!" He threw up his hands, then came out from behind the ticket booth. "You two go right on in. Be sure to see my gorgeous new sharks. They're babies now, but when they get bigger, boy, they're going to be the stars of this place."

Linc and Molly thanked Harry, then walked down a long, dark hallway, lit only by the blue light reflection of the tanks at the end. The light bounced off the walls, giving the hall an eerie quality. Families crowded the space around them, chatting happily. Friendly drawings of neon cutout cardboard fish decorated the walls, with cartoon bubbles above their heads, filled with corny knock-knock jokes that Molly could hear the kids in the aquarium repeating, with much giggling. There were miniature seahorses and whales for seats and benches, plastic eels serving as lights and conch shells holding brochures. The entire space had been designed in a fun, friendly manner, clearly oriented toward children.

Molly loved it. Every inch. And she hadn't even stepped inside the main aquarium yet.

"Why are so many children here at night?" she asked Linc.

"Vegas is a 24/7 city. That means there are round-the-clock daycare services, and parents who want a place to go with their kids when the other half is rolling the dice. This gives them a fun, entertaining place to go with the little ones."

"Oh," Molly said. "Makes sense."

The hall spilled into a forty-by-sixty-foot room, entirely encircled by glass, giving the visitor the sensation of stepping into the center of a fish tank. It reached three stories, magnificent in layers of brightly colored coral. On one side, a mini sunken galleon dominated the center of the tank, while on the other several treasure chests were piled beside a trio of smiling skeletal pirates. More friendly skeletons peppered the tank in various poses—waving at guests, dangling from a fishing line, pretending to scuba dive.

It was the kind of place every kid would love. The kind she would have loved to bring her students to see. Molly gasped. "This is incredible."

Linc grinned. "I told you. Harry loves his fish."

She spun in a circle, taking in the slow-moving sea turtles, the friendly puffer fish, the schools of silvery fish, the shy eel ducking into a dark hole at the bottom of the tank. The aquatic world was in constant motion, an underwater rainbow of activity.

Around them, children swarmed through the room, darting up to the glass to point out a bright blue fish to their mom, or to follow the path of a yellow one. Carrying above it all was the sound of laughter and the excited chatter of children having fun. Molly's hand strayed to her abdomen, and her attention dropped from the aquatic sights to the familial ones.

Would she someday bring her child to a place like this? Point out the lazy loggerhead sea turtle making a meandering circular journey? Explain why the stingray glided so effortlessly through the water? Give a quick lesson on why eels had an electric charge?

She glanced over at Linc, who had paused to watch the massive sea turtle mosey past the glass wall. Was he thinking the same thing?

"This is a great place for kids," she said to Linc.

"I guess so. I've never brought a child here."

"I think that's the best way to see this place, don't you? Through a child's eyes." She gestured toward the children all around them. "Look at how excited they are. Harry clearly geared this place toward little ones."

Linc "mmm-hmmed" her.

Not much of an answer. She tried to read his face, but couldn't. Frustrating.

"Well, I can imagine myself bringing my own children here someday," she said, hoping that statement would open a conversational door with Linc. At the very least, a *ditto*.

"I can see you doing that, too," he said.

Nothing about himself, she noted. Not a word about whether he was interested in children or not. He couldn't have said less if he'd not said a single word. She wanted to drag the answers out of him, but suspected even a tow truck couldn't do that.

Somehow, she needed to get Lincoln Curtis to open up. Needed to get him to be more conversational. She was here, after all, to get to know him, and thus far she knew exactly…zero. Clearly, what she was doing so far wasn't working. She was going to have to get more creative, and fast, if she wanted answers from Linc.

Beside her, a little girl strained to see the tank, her head bopping left to right, but her view was blocked by the taller children in front of her. Molly bent down, smiling at the cutie-pie beside her. "Want to scoot in front of me, sweetie?"

The blonde pixie grinned. "Tank-u."

Molly made way, then lowered herself to kid level. "See that up there?" She pointed to a squat yellow-and-brown-striped fish swishing his way past them. "That's a striped burrfish. Did you know they can drink a whole bunch of water, to puff their bodies out, like pufferfish do?"

The girl gasped. "Really?"

Molly glanced over to see if Linc would join in, become part of the conversation, but he was keeping his distance. Because he wasn't into kids? Or because he figured she had it all under control? "Uh-huh. They do it to scare off other animals, and when they do, those little spikes on their backs—see those?" Molly indicated the fish again. "They become really pointy and scary and say 'Don't mess with me.'"

The little girl giggled. "I bet he looks silly when he's all blowed up."

"I bet he does too. Lots of animals do silly things. That's what makes them so fun to learn about." Molly stepped back, making room for the child's mother to join them. She had a baby in a stroller, and another child holding onto one of the handles. She gave Molly a harried but grateful smile.

"Thank you for letting her in there to see the tank," the woman said. "Anna loves the aquarium."

"Me too," Molly said, shooting Anna a grin. "Enjoy the rest of the fishes."

"Thank you!" Anna trotted off, her hand in her mother's, chatting the whole time about what she'd just learned.

Linc gave Molly an approving grin when she returned to his side. "You've got a great touch with kids."

"Thanks. It's always great when they learn something—and even better when they're excited about it."

"Hopefully the software we're developing will do the same thing."

Back to work talk with him. Perhaps, though, that might be a way in to other avenues. "I think it will. I can see kids getting all charged up by the taste of information they get from playing the games in the program. Afterward, they'll want to know more." They wandered past tanks of jellyfish, glowing in the dark as they floated weightless through ebony water. "We could include things like links to aquariums and zoos. Encourage them to get out there and put that knowledge to use."

"That's a great idea." Admiration shone in his blue eyes. "That's exactly why I hired you. Because you really know this market and how to reach these kids. Then again, you work with them all day. I wouldn't know the first thing to say to one."

She laughed. "Kids are easy. They don't expect you to be a conversational giant. Just find something they're interested in—fish, sports, food—and comment on it. They'll take it from there, most times."

Linc shook his head. "You're talking to someone who spends his days talking computer code and spreadsheets with a bunch of people in suits. Not exactly the kinds of topics five-year-olds are interested in. Besides, I don't do well with kids."

"But you were a five-year-old once, right? And you've been around some, too? Nieces, nephews?"

"Yes." He gestured toward a doorway at the other side of the room. "Want to go see the sharks?"

A door had shut with Lincoln Curtis, and Molly wasn't sure why. As she followed him into the next room, she tried again. "Do you come from a big family?"

"No."

Well. A one-word answer wasn't the response she'd expected. She'd hoped to start a conversation, not bring one to a halt. How was she supposed to get to know her baby's father if he threw up a wall every time she tried to get personal?

It wasn't like she was asking for his social security number, just the basic kind of information people shared every day. Well, she wouldn't give up that easily. She was a lot more persistent than a few short sentences.

"Do you have a brother? Or a sister? I'm an only child, but always wished I had siblings."

"Harry said the new leopard shark exhibit is amazing," Linc said instead. "That might not be as crowded. Let's head over there." He let out a gust of frustration as a large group of children—probably a field trip from one of those daycares he'd mentioned—crossed in front of them in a screaming bunch. "I'm not a big fan of…crowds like this." He took her hand and zig-zagged through the maze of parents, strollers and three-foot-high bodies.

"I bet it's a big difference from what you're used to at work," she said. "But, believe me, when you're around kids long enough, they grow on you. You get used to the noise, the mess, the energy."

Like you could get used to ours, if you tried. You'd love your own, surely.

"Well, that's not something I'm planning on doing in my future."

The statement slammed into Molly, and her step faltered. *Not planning on in his future.*

Did he mean he didn't want to have children? Ever? Or just for now?

What would he say if he knew she was carrying his baby? Would he tell her he wanted it? Or would he walk away? Her fingers splayed across her still-flat belly, and she decided she wasn't ready to find that answer out. Not yet.

They emerged from the congestion of the main room into a smaller, darker room that faced one large tank, surrounded by a leopard-print frame. In the center of the tank of sharks sat a statue of a leopard, like an overgrown aquarium ornament. Linc chuckled. "Leave it to Harry to add a sense of humor to his exhibits."

Clearly she wasn't going to get anywhere with Linc, not in the area of personal topics. Either he didn't want to open up because the aquarium was so crowded, or more likely he didn't want to open up to her. Because that would mean developing a relationship, and he'd made it clear two months ago that he wasn't interested in that.

Then, she'd been glad.

Now, not so much.

Because of the baby, she told herself. Only because of the baby.

And yet…she wondered why Linc would bring her here, if he had no interest in her on a personal level? Why ask her to go on what would be considered a date by most anyone else? Why work toward developing something with her if he wasn't the kind of guy who wanted the full life, with a wife and kids?

She considered asking him. Thought better of it.

Lincoln Curtis was, after all, the exact opposite of the kind of man she wanted. Despite that one night, he was a man who lived by a schedule. Who, like her ex-husband, seemed to like everything in neat little rows and columns. After what he'd said tonight, there would clearly be no room in his life, either, for the messy chaos a child would bring.

She didn't need that again. Nor did she want to get wrapped up in someone who had stated over and over that he wasn't interested in children.

Been there, made the mistake. Got the T-shirt.

"Interesting fact about leopard sharks," Molly said, taking a couple steps closer to the tank. Talking about aquatic animals was a much better topic than talking about them. Or the lack of them. "They don't hunt, per se, but researchers have observed pairs of them swimming in the opposite direction of a school of fish. Each shark will take one flank of the school, just open their mouths, and eat to their heart's content." She turned to Linc and smiled. "Not a lot of work, but a lot of reward."

"The fish don't catch on?"

Her fingers danced against the glass. "That schooling behavior is pretty ingrained. Follow the leader…straight into the shark's mouth."

He chuckled. "Sounds like corporate life."

She watched the sharks and thought about the world Linc inhabited. Was that what had made him so jaded against the idea of children? Or was it something else, something in his past? "That world is so different from teaching kindergarten."

"Well, you're smack-dab in Corporate America now." He turned to her. "You never really told me what made you want to give up the world of small children—" he gestured toward the group of them now swarming into the room like a bunch of bees "—for corporate life? You could have just as easily stayed in San Diego and looked for another teaching job rather than coming out here to work for a software developer."

"Even though I plan to apply for new teaching jobs for next term, I thought while I'm waiting it would be nice to try something new," she said, treading carefully with her answer. Skirting as far away from the truth as possible. "And your proposal sounded really interesting."

He paused to study her. "I've told a half a dozen people about that software program, and most of them told me I was crazy. That it was a waste of company resources and time."

She shrugged. "I'm not a number cruncher like you are, but I think anything that inspires learning isn't a waste of resources." She gestured toward the children darting in and out of the room, their excited voices rising as they noticed the "dangerous" sharks. "Take Harry's aquarium. It's probably not the biggest money-maker in Vegas, but look around you. These kids are excited. They're learning. And Harry loves this place. That's a return on investment that you can't measure by a profit and loss statement."

He didn't say anything for a long time, simply watched her. She grew uncomfortable under his inquisitive gaze, sure he could read her every secret. Then Harry's voice came on the loudspeaker and announced closing time, and broke the tension between them. The room began to empty out, disappointed children reluctantly leaving.

"The children aren't the only ones learning a thing or two," Linc said quietly.

They were alone, the only sounds coming from the muted bubbling of the water in the tanks. Blue lights played across Linc's features, making him seem darker, more mysterious, and giving his eyes an almost mischievous tint.

"Who else do you mean?" Her breath caught on the words.

He took a step forward, closing the gap between them. "Why did you really come to Vegas, Molly Hunter?"

She turned her face up to meet his. Opened her mouth to tell him the truth. Closed it again, unable to get the words past her throat.

"Was it because we had unfinished business?" he asked, his voice low and as dark as the room. He reached up, caught a tendril of her hair in his hand, then let it slip through his grasp. "Because I think we do, don't you?"

She nodded, intoxicated, wrapped in his spell all over again.

Had she really ever escaped it?

No, she hadn't, and she was fooling herself if she thought she had. A hundred times—no, a thousand times—since that night, she'd pictured Linc, imagined him kissing her again, thought of how his hands had felt on her body, remembered the electric feel of his body against hers.

Her breath caught, her heart raced, and she waited, her gaze locked on his. Waiting. Anticipating. Longing. *Wanting him.*

He lowered his mouth toward hers, slowly, oh, so slowly, and she could see the future. Lincoln Curtis would kiss her. And she would do what she had done two months ago.

Fall for him.

And make the biggest mistake of her life.

Twice.

CHAPTER SIX

"I THINK I should go home," Molly said, backing away from Linc, breaking the connection before their lips met. Before he could kiss her. Before anything could happen.

If anything sent a clear message about where she stood in relation to him, those six words did. For a moment there, he'd thought—

He'd thought she'd been interested in him. Clearly he'd read her wrong. "Certainly. We both have a long day ahead of us tomorrow."

He should be glad Molly had put on the brakes before he'd kissed her and taken what wasn't a relationship down a decidedly relationship-like path. Then why did disappointment sit like a stone in his gut?

"So, what did you think of my new babies?" Harry said, coming up to both of them. His thick, white hair stuck up in a shock, but his dark blue eyes danced with excitement and enthusiasm for his aquarium and his guests. "Beautiful, aren't they? I'm thinking of adding some hammerheads in the fall. Set up a whole tool exhibit around them."

"I love your aquarium, Harry," Molly said, clearly glad for the interruption. "It's really fun. A great place to bring kids. I can see why you have so many here—it's chock-full of kid-friendly activities."

He tipped an imaginary hat Molly's way. "Why, thank you, miss. That's my goal, to make this place, and my littlest guests, feel like family. I never had any children of my own, sad to say." A shadow dropped over his face as his gaze swept across the expanse of the aquarium. "One of my biggest regrets in life. Waiting too long to get married, and being too busy to start a family. I got to enjoy this guy, though, as a kid. Him and his brother." Harry shot Linc a grin. "I remember when you got your first chemistry set. Damned near blew up the neighborhood."

"You bought me that for my birthday, if I remember right," Linc said. "You encouraged that side of me."

Harry chuckled.

Molly arched a brow. "Linc did that?"

"Oh, yes, with a little help from Marcus, I'm sure. Whenever those two boys were together, trouble was sure to follow. Linc, I suspect, was always the brains behind the operation." Harry winked. "You guys gave everyone many a laugh when you were kids. Those were some good days."

"Yeah, well, that's in the past," Linc said. "I'm too old for chemistry sets."

Harry's face softened and he put a hand on Linc's shoulder. "I miss your parents, too, Linc. They'd be proud of you if they could see you today."

Linc wondered if Harry would still say that if he knew the whole story behind Marcus's death. How Linc had let his brother down at the last minute, not been the protective older brother he'd promised to be. All Linc wanted to do right now was leave—not take a trip down Memory Lane. "Yeah, uh, thanks, Harry. And thanks again for letting us in tonight. I'll be back to see those hammerheads. I promise."

"I'll hold you to that. I miss seeing you. Be sure to bring your special lady, too," Harry said, shooting Molly a smile. "And if you're smart, my friend, you'll get a running start on your own life before it's too late."

"Appreciate the advice, but I've got a company to run." Linc clapped Harry on the shoulder.

"The company can run itself—"

"And my life can't. I know, I know."

Harry shook his head, muttered something about Linc being stubborn, then said goodbye to both of them. Once again, Linc pressed a light hand to Molly's back as they exited the building.

This time, though, she remained stiff, unyielding, beneath his touch. As if she were angry with him.

For trying to kiss her? For something he'd said?

Everything within him wanted to ask, but he told himself it was better to leave the subject alone. Getting close to Molly would only bring them back to where they had begun. To reminding him of that temporary respite from his responsibilities. To making him want something he couldn't have.

A family.

Tonight's conversations with Molly had danced around the subject of children. When she'd mentioned how much she'd like to take her own child to Harry's aquarium someday, two reactions had risen in Linc.

Worry. And envy.

Worry that she might be looking at him as a potential mate. He'd decided long ago that he was never going down the fatherhood path.

Never.

Following on the heels of the worry was an odd surge of envy. That she might someday do exactly that—with another man, and with another man's child—bothered him more than he liked to admit.

He shoved the feelings aside. He couldn't be envious of what he couldn't have. Hadn't that conversation with Harry just reminded him of the very reasons why he'd sworn off fatherhood? Better to stick to what he was good at than venture down a path he'd already failed once—

Being depended upon by those who loved him.

Outside, he hailed another cab. Once they were inside the cramped interior, Linc turned to Molly. "Listen, about what happened back there—"

"Don't worry about it," she cut in. "Neither of us wants to make another mistake."

Was that how she saw that night two months ago? As a mistake?

The cab zipped down the streets of Vegas, as alive at night as they were during the day. But Linc's mind wasn't on the brightly lit businesses or the hundreds of people streaming in and out of the casinos and restaurants along the strip.

He was lost in memories of Marcus. Of the day he'd had to go to Marcus's wife and tell her that the man she loved—the father of her children—had ended up in an early grave.

Because Linc hadn't been there to stop it. Hadn't kept his promise to be his brother's caretaker.

No, he'd been off enjoying himself on a vacation that was more of a week-long party. He'd been, in fact, too drunk to answer the phone when the first call came from Marcus. Had too many bourbons in him to do the one thing Marcus had asked—

Fill in on a conference call so Marcus could go to the doctor.

"I'm not feeling well, Linc. Yeah, yeah, I know. I can

*hear your lecture now." Marcus had let out a short laugh.
"But without you around to keep me on track, hey, I get all
distracted by the fun project of the day. And today..." His
voice had paused, strained, obvious pain in the next few
words. "Just not feeling like myself." He'd cursed, clearly
hurting. "Anyway, uh, do me a favor, and take this meeting,
will ya? Then get back to your vacation?"*

Linc hadn't gotten the phone call—instead he'd woken
up an hour later and gotten the voice mail.

Too late.

And he'd been trying to make up for that day ever since.

The cab slowed to a stop in front of Hamilton Towers.
Linc got out and held the door for Molly. As she passed
by, he caught the scent of her perfume, and the resolve he'd
solidified just a moment before crumbled a bit.

"Thank you," she said. "I really enjoyed the aquarium."

"You're welcome." They walked into the building together, and back to where they had started just a couple of
hours before—the elevators and the two choices they presented. Send Molly home to her apartment, alone, or invite
her up to his penthouse.

Linc didn't issue the invitation. He pushed the button
for up, and the doors opened almost immediately. Once
inside, he turned to her. "By the way, I don't think that night
we met was a mistake."

Her mouth opened in a tiny O of surprise. "You...you
don't?"

"Kissing you that night was...amazing. Wonderful.
Something that I would do again in a heartbeat. If..." He
let out a breath.

"If what?"

"If my life were different."

"What does that mean?"

He'd opened a can of worms he should have kept shut. "Just that I'm not the settling-down type."

"And who said I was? Or have you simply assumed you know everything there is to know about me?" She arched a defiant brow, then leaned against the wall of the elevator, her arms crossed over her chest. "So what happened to him?"

"Him...who?"

"The boy who almost blew up the neighborhood with his chemistry set? Because this Linc—" With that, she pushed off from the wall, and invaded his space and tugged at his tie. The bold, aggressive move caused his heart to accelerate. "This Linc seems to be all work and no play."

"Oh, I play," he said, his voice deep, almost a growl, his memories rocketing back to their wild night. Everything inside him wanted to kiss her, to take her in his arms again, to repeat it all.

Because he knew what she would feel like in his arms. Knew how her skin felt beneath his hands, knew the soft sounds she made when she was happy, and knew how she would curve into him afterward.

He knew it all—and as wrong as it was to want to repeat that night—

He wanted to. All the same.

"Good," she said, and a mysterious smile curved across her face, "because I will hold you to that. Very soon."

The elevator doors opened on Molly's floor, and she slipped away, leaving him disconcerted, and wondering if he should go after her. Instead, Linc watched her walk away, then waited for the doors to close again. In moments, he was on the top floor, in his penthouse apartment. Alone.

And telling himself for the ten thousandth time that he had made the right decision. The only one he could make.

* * *

Molly flipped through the pages of the *Memories for Your Baby* journal she'd bought at a bookstore earlier that morning, and realized how few of the blanks she could fill in. She knew more about Lincoln Curtis's occupation and company than what made him tick. She'd filled in what she could—father's eye color, hair color, height—but the pages with "Earliest Childhood Memory," "Favorite Food," "Dreams for the Future," and so many more, lay blank.

She'd had a peek inside Linc the man last night at the aquarium, but the moment had been brief, as if he'd wanted to be sure not to expose too much. Not to allow anyone into his heart.

She'd been in Vegas for several days, and had made plenty of progress on the software—

And little to no progress with Linc, except for the brief snippets of information she'd gleaned last night. Molly let out a sigh of frustration, thinking of all the pages that had yet to be filled in. How was she supposed to get to know the father of her baby? She couldn't very well leave those pages blank. What was she going to tell her baby when he or she was old enough to start asking questions? *Go do a Google search on your dad?* No. That would never do.

She had to find a way to get Linc to open up. That was the only answer. The problem was how, without seeming like a stalker or someone interested in him.

Because she wasn't. Not in the least.

Well, maybe not *entirely*.

She put the book into her tote bag, then pulled out a hand mirror and checked her appearance. Her gaze lighted on her lips, on the mouth Linc had almost—*almost*—kissed last night.

Until she'd stopped him.

Her fingers fluttered to her mouth, and her mind drifted back two months to the last time Linc had kissed her. The moment so thrilling, so incredible, it had chased all coherent thought from her head. How she craved another kiss like that. And another, and another.

But, oh, if she crossed that line again, where would that take her? Back down the same crazy path as before. No. She couldn't do that.

She had a new priority now, one that didn't involve a relationship with Lincoln Curtis. Back at the aquarium, he'd made it clear he wasn't interested in settling down and raising kids. He wasn't even interested in children at all.

If that was so, Molly thought, as she put away the mirror and headed down the hall toward the R & D room, then why was he so invested in a software program directed toward children? It made no sense. Lincoln Curtis was a paradox, a man who presented one face one day, and another the next.

Which man was he? The one she'd met in the bar, the one she'd fallen for? Or the no-nonsense CEO with no room in his life for so much as a potted plant?

Molly pushed on the door to R & D and entered the room. "Good morning," Molly said to Roy. "You're in early."

"I like being here when it's quiet. No one around to interrupt me, no phones ringing. In an hour or two, this place will be swarming. Makes it hard to concentrate sometimes." Roy put down his coffee cup and slid into the chair behind the computer. "We made good progress yesterday. Jerome is out sick, so I was thinking—"

"I'd like to work with Linc all day today," she said, the idea forming as fast as the words left her mouth. Why hadn't she thought of it earlier?

Roy's jaw dropped. "Mr. Curtis?"

"This whole thing is his idea, after all. I think he needs to have more input than he has so far."

"Uh, okay. Good luck with that," he said. "Have you seen his schedule?"

"I have."

"You do know that he lives and dies by those little blocks of time, right? Not to burst your bubble, Molly, but I've worked here for six years and I have never seen Mr. Curtis take so much as an afternoon off to go play golf, and he loves golf. He makes the rest of us feel guilty for calling in sick when we have the flu."

But Linc had taken a couple of hours off the day she'd arrived in town. That told her he could be talked into the concept. And he'd once been the adventurous boy with the chemistry set. She fully intended to bring out that side of him again. That, she suspected, was the key to getting him to open up.

"We'll see about that." Molly grabbed her purse, then headed out of the room and up to the twentieth floor. She'd do this for the baby's sake, she told herself. Not because she was curious. Not because every time she looked into his blue eyes her heart skipped a beat. Not because seeing him again had reawakened the nearly electric attraction she'd felt that night, and had her wondering about the Linc she'd met—the sexy, fun, engaging man who'd swept her off her feet. Literally.

Molly strode down the end of the hall. Because it was still early—barely past seven-thirty in the morning—many of the offices were still empty. Even Linc's assistant hadn't arrived yet. A light blazed in Linc's office—not a big surprise—and Molly headed toward his door.

Then her gaze lit on a matching door to the right. Marcus Curtis, Vice President.

Linc's brother, the one Harry had mentioned last night. Of course.

Molly thought of the journal in her bag. Who better to tell her about Linc than his own brother? Perhaps Marcus Curtis wouldn't be as closed off as Lincoln. Surely he had plenty of memories of Linc to share. She crossed to the second office, raised her hand and knocked.

No answer.

She knocked again, a little harder this time, and heard a voice on the other side, saying, she thought, "Come in." She opened the door, and entered the room. A man stood at the window, his back to her.

"Mr. Curtis? I'm Molly Hunter. I work for Lincoln and—"

The man wheeled around. "What the hell are you doing in here?"

"Linc." Molly stumbled to a stop. Had she accidentally walked into the wrong office? "I'm sorry. I was looking for your brother and I thought—"

"My brother isn't here." He crossed the room in three short strides, fury emanating from him in palpable waves. "What could you possibly want with my brother?"

"I…" Molly's voice trailed off. What could she tell him? Certainly not the truth. She looked from Linc to the empty desk, confused. Where was Marcus Curtis? Why was Linc in here? And why was he so angry? "I…I wanted to get his input on the software program. I mean, he went to the same summer camp as you did and I thought—"

"You *didn't* think, Molly. Or ask anyone. You just barged in here." Linc's voice was harsh, the edges of his words sharp. "My brother is dead. So he can't answer your questions. Or for that matter, mine."

Then Linc brushed past her and out of the room.

* * *

Well. He hadn't handled that very well. At all. He'd attacked Molly, and for something that wasn't her fault.

It wasn't like there was a sign outside of Marcus's door, saying "deceased." His brother's office looked the same today as it had the last time Marcus had walked through those doors. As if Marcus was going to show up tomorrow at Curtis Systems, the same familiar goofy grin on his face, a ready joke on his lips, and take his place at the conference table.

Linc's gaze strayed to the photo of his brother on the wall. Marcus's wide grin dominated the image, so evocative of his younger brother's spirit. Devil-may-care, live-for-the-moment, put responsibility aside at every possible juncture to grab a moment of fun.

And where had that gotten him?

Linc shook his head, shoving the thoughts to the back of his mind. Then he pushed aside the work on his desk, got to his feet, and went in search of Molly. He'd been wrong, and he needed to do something to make it right again.

He found her just outside the R & D room, her hand on the doorknob, about to enter. "Molly."

She turned toward him, and the war of emotions on her face—anger, hurt, disappointment—said it all. He'd been a jerk. He cleared his throat. "I'm sorry about how I acted back there. I just didn't expect to find anyone in my brother's office. It's just…" Linc let out a breath. "It's just been very hard on me since he died."

Understatement of the year.

"I'm so sorry, Linc." Her features softened and she took a step toward him. Her hand lighted on his arm, a sympathetic, soothing touch. "I can only imagine how hard it must have been to lose someone you love like that. From what Harry said, Marcus must have been a wonderful person."

Pain arced in his chest, and he swallowed hard. He could

see the unasked question in her eyes, the one that would tear that wound further.

How did he die?

No. He wouldn't go there. Not now. Not ever. Linc broke the contact between them. "I just wanted to stop by to apologize. I won't keep you. I'm sure Roy is waiting for you—"

She shook her head, cutting off his sentence. "Actually, I told him I was planning on spending the day with you."

He blinked. "With me?"

"You've been Mr. Invisible since we started this, and while your notebook has been a great start, it's not the same as having you." She eyed him. "This is your dream, Linc. You can't just hand it off to other people and expect them to fulfill it."

She wanted him to be involved? Hadn't he already made it clear over a week ago that he didn't need to be a part of this? He'd given her his notes, after all. What more did she need? "I can certainly stop in throughout the day and offer suggestions."

That was all. Don't ask for anything more.

But she didn't read his thoughts. "Not good enough. I want more."

He arched a brow. "More?"

"If there's one thing I've learned as a teacher, it's that students learn best in a visual setting. I'm your student on this, and I want you to show me."

"Show you?" What was she suggesting? "How? Where? When?"

"Today, now, with me." She laughed, the sound light as spring rain. "Take the day off, Linc, and come with me."

He stared at her. The words reverberated in his head,

so…foreign, he almost couldn't comprehend them. *"Take the day off?"*

Another tinkling of laughter escaped Molly. "Are you just going to repeat everything I say?" A tease lit her eyes. "Yes, the whole day. Off, as in no work, from here until tomorrow. Don't tell me you've never done that."

"Honestly, I can't remember the last time I did." That was a lie. He could remember. Three years ago this past April. He'd taken a week off, at Marcus's suggestion, and gone off on one of those adventure vacations. Two days into his vacation—

And he'd had to jet back to deliver the worst possible news to Marcus's widow.

Linc shook his head. "Molly—"

"The company won't fall apart if you take one day off. I'm positive of that."

What was it with this woman? Why did she keep trying to push him to do the very things he avoided? Didn't she understand it wasn't just about taking the day off?

It was about entering the world that Molly inhabited. The one of ordinary people. People who lived in picket-fenced houses, with dogs and kids. People who could put everything aside at a moment's notice—

And rent a room in a hotel in Vegas with a stranger. And imagine falling in love with that stranger, having a life with her. A future.

Molly cocked her head and flashed him a smile. "So what do you say, Lincoln Curtis? Wanna play hooky?"

Everything within him wanted to say no, knew he should say no, just at the thought of the sheer logistics involved in rearranging his schedule, but then his gaze met hers, and the teasing flirtation sparkling in her green eyes. In an instant, he was back in that bar with her, and she was looking at him exactly the same way, seeing Linc, not Lincoln Curtis, but Linc.

For just one night, he'd felt freedom. From his life. From his job. From the relentless tight yoke of his responsibilities, but most of all, from the burden of guilt that had weighed heavier than two anvils on his shoulders for all these years. And imagined something different.

Play hooky, she'd asked. It was like giving himself a temporary pardon, with a beautiful woman by his side.

"Yes," he said, before his better judgment could override his decision.

CHAPTER SEVEN

LAKE MEAD sprawled in front of them, more than two hundred square miles of deep blue beauty, sparkling in the bright sunshine. Boats and kayaks dotted the lake, while swimmers and sunbathers populated the rocky shore. In the far distance, the Hoover Dam's massive wall held the gallons and gallons of water in place, while craggy rock formations in soft hues of terra-cotta, pale yellow and purple, surrounded the lake, as if Mother Nature had painted her own natural barrier from the world.

"It's beautiful," Molly said on a breath. "Absolutely amazing. When I picked this place from the brochure, I had no idea it would be so wonderful in person."

"I haven't been here in forever. My parents used to take us here when we were kids, nearly every weekend in the summer," Linc said. "I'd forgotten how beautiful it was."

But he wasn't talking about the lake. He meant Molly—

And she had no idea.

Sunshine lit Molly's hair from above, casting golden tones over the dark brown tresses, making her seem kissed by the rays themselves. A soft smile held steady on her face, as if happiness had taken hold deep inside her and refused to let go. She wore a floral skirt today, and a plain eyelet white top, a summery, simple outfit that took years off her age and made him, in his suit and tie, feel old and set in his ways beside her. Everything about Molly screamed carefree, happy, light.

The exact opposite of him.

She intrigued him. Mystified him.

"Come on," Molly said, putting out her hand. "Let's go down to the water."

Linc glanced at her, then at the lake lapping gently along the shore. "I'm not exactly dressed for that."

She tossed him a grin. "Then get that way." She bent down, slipped off her low-heeled shoes and tossed them to the side. Her bare feet sank into the sand between the big stones peppering the beach, with only her red polished toes peeking out like a tease. Then she propped a fist on her hip and waited for him to do the same. When he hesitated, she laughed. "Yes, Linc, take off your shoes. Roll up the cuffs of that gazillion-dollar suit. And let's walk on the beach. I promise, you won't melt. You might get wet, but you'll live."

He thought of arguing, of saying he could certainly tell her about his experiences at camp and his ideas for the software without having to get barefoot, but then a sudden, crazy urge rose inside him. The same one that had spurred him into the hotel bar that night, and made him open up to a perfect stranger.

To be a part of the playful, carefree attitude that surrounded Molly like a cloud. She stood there, smiling at him, waiting, expecting him to join her.

And so Lincoln Curtis, multi-millionaire CEO owner of one of the top software companies in the country, bent down, unlaced his Ferragamo dress shoes, kicked them into the sand, then rolled up the cuffs of his tailor-made suit and headed down to the water's edge with Molly.

The delicate sandpipers darted away as they neared, but the staid mallard ducks kept on swimming in steady circles, unaffected by the human presence. Every once in a while, one would dip under the surface of the water for a quick fish snack. It was all so ordinary, so out of Linc's normal realm that he felt as if he'd jetted to another planet.

Beneath his feet, the soft, damp sand was cool. A light breeze whispered across his face, danced along his bare legs, while the sun warmed his face and back. God, he'd forgotten how good it felt just to be outside.

He reached out and took Molly's hand in his, the connection so natural it was as if she'd always been by his side. He wanted more, wanted to crush her to his chest, wanted to kiss her, but for now he simply held her hand and enjoyed the beach. And Molly.

"Tell me what would make a child want to learn more about a place like this. A child like you used to be," Molly said.

He chuckled. "You mean, what would make them put aside their books—or in my case, spreadsheets and conference calls—and take time to get down in the dirt, so to speak, here?"

"Yes."

"I'm not sure I know." He glanced out at the blue expanse of water, searching for an answer in the vast depths of Lake Mead. "Sometimes, when you spend day after day behind the glass walls of an office, you forget what the real world is like. What it's like to have the sun on your face, the sand and rocks under your feet. What it's like to just…be."

"But you're wealthy," she said. "Surely you must take vacations to exotic locations, with luxury hotels and miles of beaches. Places with lots more sand than this."

He snorted. "Money doesn't always equal freedom."

Molly cocked her head and studied him, waiting, he knew, for him to elaborate.

He didn't.

Instead he released her and picked up one of the hundreds of rocks littering the beach. He bounced it in his palm, then turned toward Molly. "Do you see those rock croppings out there in the water?" He pointed toward a long, multi-colored line of rocks that snaked into the lake, like fingers.

She nodded.

"They date back all the way to the Paleozoic and Mesozoic age. They've shifted and moved over the years, because of the movement of the tectonic plates running beneath us, which is what gives them all those fault lines. That means even this rock—" he turned it over in his hand "—could go all the way back to the dinosaur age."

She bent down and picked up a second rock. "How cool. And interesting."

"I look at those stacks of rocks, and think about how long they've been there, in that same place. When I was a kid, I read books about rocks. That's how I learned about these ones, actually. It was in a book I got for my eighth birthday. I even had a rock collection at one time. My dad used to travel a lot for his job, and he'd bring me home a rock from whatever city he'd been in."

"Why rocks?"

He thought a moment. "They're steady. They don't change, not unless some massive force of nature impacts them."

"Like you?"

"Me?" He chuckled. "I'm not that bad."

She started walking along the shore, with him keeping pace alongside her. Molly stepped along the water's edge, the lake ebbing in and out and dancing with her delicate feet. "I don't know you very well," she said, "but if you ask me, it doesn't take a rocket scientist to see that in real life you're about as relaxed as a brick."

He'd been about to talk about the marvels of geological formations, about the incredible handiwork of Mother Nature, when Molly's statement dropped a surprise into the conversation. "In my real life?"

She paused and caught his gaze. "I don't count that night in the bar as our real lives. Do you?"

Her emerald gaze held so many questions, ones he hadn't even answered for himself. A part of him ached to reach out and touch her, to draw her into his arms and end all discussion of rocks and lives and who each of them really were. But he didn't. "When you're the boss, there's a lot of stress on your shoulders. If I don't seem relaxed, it's because I'm not."

"But you were that night," she persisted.

"A temporary condition, sort of like a twenty-four-hour flu," he said, tossing off the words like a joke. "Now, back to the software. I think something like these rocks would really interest kids. They're like…dinosaur rocks." He tossed the stone back onto the ground. "When I was a kid, I read every book on geology I could get my hands on. Then my dad brought me home that rock collection, and suddenly what I'd seen on the page was real. I wanted to get out there and find more of those rocks in real life for myself. That's the kind of thing I want other kids to find. They'll use the software, and that will whet their appetite—"

"For kicking off their shoes and walking in the sand?" Molly finished for him.

"Exactly. So if we make the program interactive, with activities that encourage them to go outside, and employ what they learn on the screen in the real world—"

"It'll become a program that makes them truly interact with the world."

"Exactly. Don't just click through stuff on dinosaur rocks, go out and look for some." Linc veered away from the beach, and headed back up the shore. "Did you get what you needed? I should get back to the office."

"You're not very good at this, are you?" She laughed, then bent down and picked up their shoes, handing his to him, and tucking hers under her arm. She reached out and grabbed his arm, and started leading him back to the parking lot. "I have no intentions of letting you go back to work. In fact, think of this as a kidnapping. An all-day adventure kidnapping."

The smile on her face, and the way she had taken charge, both physically and verbally, sent a thrill through him. For so many years he'd been the caretaker, the boss, the one telling everyone else what to do. The decision-maker. To have Molly step up and tell him she was taking that responsibility off his shoulders—no arguments allowed—was intoxicating.

He grinned, and allowed her to lead him through the parking lot and back to the town car. "Where are we going?"

"That, Linc, is for me to know, and you to find out." She winked, and Lincoln Curtis, the man whose days always followed a schedule, put his future temporarily in the hands of another.

Molly Hunter barely recognized herself.

It wasn't the "I Heart Nevada" T-shirt she'd bought and changed into, or the new hot-pink flip-flops she'd exchanged for her sandals. It was this new, take-charge persona who had dragged Lincoln Curtis off to the marina on the other side of Lake Mead, told him to go into the gift shop, buy a change of clothes and then rent a boat so they could spend the afternoon out on the water.

Who was this person? And why was it that every time she got around Linc, she became so much…wilder?

At some point, she'd gone beyond pumping him for information about his personal life, and become…the woman she'd been that night she'd met him. She had to remember to tread carefully. To not get off-track.

That could lead to so much trouble—and another bad decision. One she couldn't afford, not right now. Not ever.

"I look like a tourist," Linc said as he joined her on the deck. He'd exchanged his business clothes for khaki shorts, a light blue T-shirt with a Lake Mead logo on the pocket, and a pair of boat shoes.

She laughed. "I think that's the point." She reached forward, and patted the logo on his chest. "I like this look. It suits you."

He glanced down. "You think so?"

She nodded. "Not that I don't like your suits, but this makes you seem more like…" She paused. "Like the man I first met."

Had she really said that? She hadn't intended to let those words slip out. Must be because her mind kept skipping back to that night, like a record with a stuck needle. She forced herself to look away, to concentrate on the boat.

The captain nodded toward them, then started the engine. It roared to life, then reduced to a *gurgle-gurgle*. Linc and Molly took up seats on the plush white bench at the rear of the boat. In seconds, they were off, cruising the massive lake at a leisurely speed, a gentle breeze offsetting the relentless Nevada sun. Her stomach protested a little, but Molly nibbled on the crackers she'd bought in the gift shop.

"Not much of a nutritious lunch," Linc said, gesturing toward the crackers.

"I, uh, had a big breakfast." That was all she needed—

to have to explain to him why she was feeling nauseous. He didn't press her, just seemed to accept her answer.

"You know, I own a boat," Linc said. "A yacht, actually. I've never even been on it. I bought it a few years ago with good intentions that never got fulfilled."

"So it's just sitting there, in the water?"

"In dry dock. Waiting for me to find the time."

"I love the water," Molly said. "I've always wanted a boat. Never mind a yacht. But neither is exactly possible on a teacher's salary."

"Then maybe someday I'll take you out on mine."

She heard the words, the promise, and wondered if Linc really meant it, or if it was just one of those offhand comments that people make to be polite. A thrill went through her nonetheless, coupled with an image of a future—one with her and Linc together, out on the water, enjoying the day. And each other.

"That would be nice," she said quietly. "Very nice."

The boat slowed to a stop in the center of the lake, and the captain dropped the anchor, then cut the engine. "If you all want to fish for a while, it's a great day for it." He rose, and grabbed two skinny red fishing poles from a mounting bracket on the port side of the boat. "I've got some bait down below, too."

Linc took the poles, handing one to Molly, while the captain ducked down into the galley of the boat to retrieve some drinks and the canister of bait. "I think we need to have the entire boating experience, don't you?"

She grinned. "Absolutely. It's research, after all."

He returned the smile. "Always work, work, work with you."

She laughed. "My goodness, Lincoln Curtis. Did you just make a joke? About work?"

He chuckled. "Seems I did. You bring out the worst in me."

"Or is it the best?" She flashed him another grin, and as she did, she realized something—

She was flirting with him.

At some point she had shifted gears from her mission of getting to know her baby's father to a new one of wanting to get close to Linc again, to the Linc she had first met, the one who had intrigued her and made her explore an entirely new side of herself. She'd stopped listening for clues to his past, to the answers she needed for the journal, and instead begun to look for clues to…

To whether he was interested in her, too.

He looked over at her, caught her watching him fiddling with the fishing rod, and sent her a teasing grin, the exact same one that she had seen that first night. A quiver of heat raced through her belly. The fishing pole slipped out of her hands and tumbled to the floor of the boat.

Linc came up beside her to reach for it, just as the boat shifted with a wave from a passing boat's wake. The sudden unsteadiness tossed Linc against her. His chest collided with hers, and he curved one arm around her back, before they teetered back to a steady position.

He glanced down at her. "I'm sorry."

"That's okay. It was the…" Words escaped her for a second. "The water. Or…the boat."

"Or…not."

Heat curled between them, and the unmistakable whisper of desire rose in the air. Molly opened her mouth to say something witty, something to defuse the tension, but nothing came to mind.

She could barely breathe, never mind think. All she saw, all she knew, was Linc's touch. The intensity of his blue eyes on hers. The warmth of his body against her skin. She molded into him, as naturally as ivy curling around a tree, as if she had always been in his arms.

As if no time at all had passed since the last time they'd touched. Kissed. Made love.

Linc reached up and captured her jaw in his palm. "Oh, Molly," he said, his voice gruff, deep. "What are you doing to me?"

Her breath caught in her throat, her heart raced.

Then he leaned forward, and with no help from the boat, closed the gap between them, and kissed her.

CHAPTER EIGHT

KISSING Molly Hunter was like the perfect symphony. Every touch, every moment, hit the exact note, as if she'd been made just for him. Her satiny lips skated across his, and her body curved against him, molding exactly into his frame. Wanting more of her, no, wanting *all* of her, Linc wrapped his arm tighter around Molly's waist, then tangled the other hand in the silky lengths of her hair, and deepened their kiss.

God, he had missed her. Missed the taste of her, a mixture of sweet and spicy, like apples and coffee. Missed the soft sounds that escaped her when his tongue dipped in to tease hers. Missed the feel of her hourglass figure against his body.

But most of all, missed the way she could, with one kiss, make him forget everything in his life and open that window of hope, if only for a moment, that he could have it all.

She drew back, her face flushed, and smiled at him. Her dark green gaze seemed to go on forever, and he wondered if it was possible for a man to lose himself in those emerald depths. "That was…incredible."

He returned the smile. "I agree."

"And…a complication." The smile faltered, and she

slipped out of his grasp to put some distance between them. A whisper of cool air worked its way into the vacated space. "We're working together, Linc. That's all."

He reached out, trailed a finger along her jaw, wanting to kiss her again more than anything. His better sense told him she had done the right thing, but right now, he wasn't in any mood to listen. "Really? Because it doesn't seem like we've done anything resembling work all day."

A beat passed. "So what are we doing?"

He cupped her jaw, his thumb teasing along her lower lip, touching what his mouth couldn't. "What if it wasn't just about work?"

What was he doing? He had no time, nor room for a relationship. He was, in fact, the last man on earth who should try to have a relationship with a woman like her.

Yet, ever since he'd met Molly, he'd danced around the thought of having her in his life. At first for a night—

Now for longer.

Impossible. He couldn't. Not now. Not ever. And especially not with a woman who clearly wanted the whole package—a husband, a family, a picket fence.

With any other man, she could have that. But not with Lincoln Curtis.

"Take care of your brother, Linc. Watch out for him. He's fragile, and he needs someone to take care of him."

And then, when Marcus was dying—

"Take care of my family. They're depending on you now."

"Are you saying you want us to…date?" Molly asked.

He should say no. Everything inside him geared up to vocalize that word, but then he took in her heart-shaped face, the question in her green eyes, the faint flush of fresh desire in her face, and opened his mouth instead to say—

"Well, here's your bait," the captain said, thrusting a

small white container toward them. Holes had been poked in the top, and a dusting of dirt coated the rim. "Worms. Big, fat, juicy ones, too."

"Great," Linc said. Gee, if anything could kill the mood, those five words could.

"Fish love 'em," the captain went on, oblivious to what he had interrupted. "Now, if you're a little on the squeamish side, I can put them on the hook for you." His grin revealed a couple of missing teeth. "All part of the service."

Molly's face, however, had turned positively green. She backed up, grabbed her fishing pole and handed it to the captain, staying as far from the bait as possible.

Any remaining sexual tension that had been hovering in the air disappeared. The moment was over. Molly couldn't have been any clearer about that if she'd hung up a billboard.

Linc refused to call the sinking feeling in his gut disappointment.

"Fishing's all about patience," the captain said as he worked the wriggling worm onto the curve of the hook. Molly averted her gaze until the deed was done, and the captain had given her back her pole. "But a good catch is always worth it in the end. Young people always expect the fish to just jump on out of the lake and right into their hands." The captain let out a laugh. "Life ain't like that, and neither is fishing."

Linc baited his own hook while the captain went on with his homilies and fishing analogies, filling the dead air between Linc and Molly. Probably a good thing.

What would Linc have said just then to the dating question? He would have said yes, even if it was the wrong answer. He wanted to date Molly. He wanted to explore this relationship. See where it led. He wanted to expand the narrow channel of his life to include her, too.

But what he wanted and what he should do were two completely different things. Molly was, as the captain would say, a good catch, but one Linc shouldn't be fishing for, no matter how tempting the thought.

As he slipped into place beside Molly and lowered his line into the water while trying to block out the captain's endless chatter, he thought back to the night in the aquarium. To how easily Molly had connected with that little girl. She'd made it seem so effortless, almost...

Magical.

He'd seen the joy on the little girl's face as they shared a giggle over the burrfish, and felt an odd sense of longing. All around them, there'd been families—husbands, wives, mothers and fathers and children who had managed to create a complete circle.

Once, he had thought he could have that. Then Marcus had died—

And Linc had decided his efforts were better spent behind a desk than standing at an altar making a promise he wasn't sure he could keep.

Beside him, Molly suddenly let out a gasp.

"Ooh! I think I have a bite." She jerked on her pole, and the bright yellow-and-pink bobber disappeared beneath the water's surface. She started to reel in the line, the rod clicking with the movement of the handle, watching the taut filament as it drew closer and closer to the boat. Then the line suddenly went slack and drooped into the water. "Oh, no. I think I lost him."

"Sometimes that's what happens," the captain said. "Despite your best work, the good ones get away." He gestured to her to keep on reeling in the line. "We'll just bait her up again and keep trying."

Molly let the captain re-bait her hook, and in a moment

had her line back in the water. They fished for a while longer, with little results. The breeze that had been just enough to offset the relentless August sun dropped to a whisper, and the temperature rose. Soon, the fishing trip became less about fun and more about trying to stay cool.

"I think I've had enough fishing," Molly said, as she reeled in her line, then rested her pole against the side of the boat. She turned to Linc, that devilish smile back on her face. "Want to go for a dip?"

"Swimming?" He tried to think of the last time he'd done that, and couldn't. The idea sparked an immediate image of seeing Molly in a bathing suit. "Trying to work in the full lake experience in one day?"

"Oh, yes, I want to try everything." A twinkle lit her eyes, and for the second time that day, Linc wondered if she was flirting with him. Hell, he didn't wonder. He knew.

Desire roared through his veins. This was a dangerous game, one he shouldn't play, but when she flirted with him like that, it rocketed him right back to that night two months ago, and every resolution he'd made melted in the power of her smile.

"Come on, Linc. If you're going to take a day off, do it right." She reached forward, took his fishing pole out of his hands, reeled it in and rested it in the holder on the side of the boat. Once again, Molly took charge, surprising him. Enticing him. "You can swim, right? You haven't left your swimming skills in dry dock, too?"

He laughed. "Not at all. I may be a little rusty, but I won't drown."

"Good. Though I do know CPR." Her grin quirked up higher on one side than the other, and the double entendre charged the air between them, raising the temperature more than the sun ever could.

"Maybe I'll flounder just a little," Linc said. "Just so you can practice on me."

She laughed. "Putting your life in my hands? Very brave indeed."

"That's me, always living on the edge."

Her laughter exploded out of her now, and he found himself joining in, feeling lighter than he had in days. Months. Was this what it could be like? If he opened his life to something permanent? Allowed himself to have what everyone else did?

"I'm going to go change into my swimsuit before I melt in this heat," Molly said. "Meet you back on the deck?"

"Definitely."

While Molly changed, the captain climbed into his deck chair, dropped a ball cap over his face, and fell asleep, leaving Linc and Molly, for all intents and purposes, alone. A moment later, Linc heard a sound behind him and turned.

Oh. Boy.

Linc swallowed hard. Told himself to breathe.

Molly stood there in a two-piece dark blue bathing suit that skimmed over her curves and accentuated every part of her that he liked best, while also exposing the sweet expanse of peach skin along her belly. She seemed self-conscious about it, though, and kept a hand splayed across her stomach. The suit wasn't so revealing that it would end up in the center of one of those sports magazines, which made it all the more perfect. He loved the juxtaposition between sweet and spicy, the temptation to see more than what was covered up.

"You look…incredible," he said. Managed, really. "Stunning."

She blushed. "I…well, thank you." The palm stayed on her belly and she turned slightly away from him. When she did, he noticed she had put on a little weight since the last time he'd seen her. Not much, just a little, most of it showing along her waist. Was that what she was embarrassed about? If so, no need, because she looked beautiful to him.

"Give me thirty seconds to change," Linc said. He took a second look at her. "Make that ten." He dashed down below, exchanged his shorts and T for the swimsuit he'd bought in one of the Lake Mead gift shops, then hurried back up to the deck.

Molly laughed. "That was fast."

"I had incentive." He wanted to take her in his arms again, wanted to feel her warm skin against his own, but knew that doing so would take things up several notches. Were they ready for that? More, was he ready for that?

Or should he be smart, and keep the brakes on?

Before he could decide, Molly swung her legs over the side of the boat, stepped onto the small platform at the back, and dove into the water, in one smooth, effortless motion. She disappeared in the deep blue depths.

He followed her, the heat of the day evaporating the instant his body met the cool water of the lake. He dove down several feet, then broke through the surface, a little ways from Molly. She treaded water beside him, grinning. Her dark hair hung in a sleek curtain down her back, and water droplets kissed her face, hung in tantalizing teardrops along her lips.

"You were right. This is much better than fishing," he said.

"Much," she agreed. "And better than working?"

He chuckled. "Yes. Definitely."

He thought of all the days he'd spent in his office. Not just weekdays, but Saturdays, Sundays. Late nights, early mornings. While his employees took off for lake vacations, cruises, beach trips with their families. Entire days went by where Linc didn't notice the sun rise or set, because he'd arrived too early and left too late, starting and ending his day in darkness.

Was this what he'd been missing? This…sense of freedom?

He'd had good reasons for doing so, but still, a feeling of loss dropped in his gut. He thought of what Harry had said, and wondered—

Would he look back on those years later in his life with satisfaction, because he had done what was expected of him? Or regret, because he had put aside the very things everyone else had?

Today, he'd had a taste of that. It wasn't just the water, but the way the entire day had unfolded, with no schedule, no rules. Molly had suggested something and they'd done it, for as long as they'd wanted, then moved on to something else. He hadn't even realized until now that he hadn't missed his cell phone—

Because he'd left it in the car with Saul.

Accidentally, he'd thought at the time. Perhaps more on purpose than he'd realized.

"You should try playing hooky more than once in your life, Mr. Straight and Narrow," Molly said, sending a splash of water his way. "Who knows? Taking a day off every once in a while might be good for you."

"Oh, yeah?" He returned the splash, but she ducked out of the way, and swam a foot to his right. "How so?"

"It's called recharging your batteries, Mr. Curtis. It's all the rage." She grinned.

Yes, she was definitely flirting with him.

And more, he was flirting back. And enjoying it. Immensely.

When was the last time he'd flirted with a woman? Really flirted like this?

The answer came swiftly. Two months ago. With this very same woman. Before that…he couldn't remember. That alone was a clear sign he was spending too much time behind his desk. He might not be interested in a long-term committed relationship, but being alone—

Not exactly good for him, either.

He tossed Molly a grin. "Then I'll be sure to add free time into my schedule."

She laughed. "You can't do that, silly. It's not fun then. You have to just—" she swam up to him, lifting her chin toward his, the sun sparkling like gold dust in her eyes "—do it."

Do it. Oh, he wanted to. And do a hell of a lot more than just take a day off.

The temptation to kiss her again roared through him, and he leaned forward to do that, but she darted away, teasing him. "Then who will run the company?"

"You have people. Let them do their jobs."

"Can't. If some of my *people* are playing hooky with me." He splashed her lightly again, and kicked twice, bringing his body right beside hers.

She considered that, putting a finger to her lips, as if deep in thought, and Linc thought he had never enjoyed a playful expression on a woman's face as much as he did hers. "True. Then maybe you should take advantage of the opportunities closer to home. Like that amazing pool at Hamilton Towers. I haven't had time to try it out yet, but it looks fabulous. I bet you love it."

"There's a pool at Hamilton Towers?" He tried to think if he'd ever journeyed to the courtyard, or for that matter anywhere past the lobby of the building and his apartment. He'd simply moved in—or rather had the movers handle the move—because he'd been, surprise, surprise, at work. What other amenities had he missed in the building?

She laughed. "You haven't noticed the pool? It's amazing. All set in this grove of palm trees and boulders, like a cozy lagoon hideaway." She tossed him another teasing smile. "Very decadent."

Right now, the word *decadent* was swirling around something other than the pool in Linc's mind. His gaze focused on her smile, then the tease in her eyes, and the desire he'd tried so hard to ignore charged through his veins, undeniable, unstoppable.

He gave up trying to resist the insistent urges pounding inside him and captured Molly's waist in his hands, pulling her against him. Her eyes widened, her mouth opened in a little O of surprise. Their legs swished together under the water in a sensuous, slippery dance that brought back every memory of the night they'd spent together.

Want roared through his veins, hammered in his head. His grip tightened around her waist. He wanted more than what they could do in the water—he wanted to be back in the Bellagio, with nothing but hours ahead and Molly lying beside him, smiling that incredible smile.

"I think this is pretty decadent," Linc said. "Don't you?"

"Yes," she said, the word escaping her on a breath.

"And something we probably shouldn't do."

"Yes. It could lead to…complications."

"Exactly." But right now, he didn't care about the complications. They seemed a million miles away. His hands slid along her waist, and then up her back, along silky, soft skin, drawing her even closer to him. "Let's complicate things, Molly," he said, then he stopped worrying about what he shouldn't do, and did what he wanted to do.

And kissed her again.

* * *

Somewhere, Molly had lost track of her good intentions. She'd thought she knew what she was doing when she'd asked Linc to take the day off. Thought she had a good plan when she'd dragged him to Lake Mead with a day of outdoor adventures planned.

Instead, she found the one taking the adventure was her heart.

Oh, this was so not the plan.

But as Linc kissed her again, she couldn't seem to find the wherewithal to get back to the plan.

Or, for that matter, remember what it was.

Coupled with the whisper of the water against their skin, the entire experience only heightened her desire for him, raised the attraction she'd felt that first night to a whole new level. Her hands gripped his back, clutching at the muscles bunching beneath his skin as he moved to hold her tighter, pull her even further into his embrace. Her breasts crushed into his chest, but she wanted more, wanted him to touch every inch of her, to take them back to that night they'd spent together.

God, she wanted him. She'd always wanted him.

His tongue slid into her mouth, dancing with hers, stoking an already burning fire. One of his hands danced up her side, setting every nerve on fire, then came around to cup her breast through the thin fabric of her swimsuit. She arched against him, wanting more, wanting nothing more right now than for Linc to tug off the skimpy top and end this constant need for him. His fingers snaked beneath the fabric and captured her breast, roaming across the sensitive nipple. She moaned, pressing her pelvis to his, to the unmistakable erection that told her he was just as affected as she was. Rational thought disappeared. Their legs tangled in and out as they trod water, bobbed up and down.

Every beat of her heart, every breath she took, began and ended with Linc's touch, his kiss.

Then he pulled back just long enough to murmur her name against her mouth in a ragged breath, and she thought she would come completely undone. She was falling for him—oh, God, she was falling for him in a huge, huge way.

"God, Molly, what are we doing?" he said, his voice hoarse, his body hard and tense. Everything within her wanted to touch him, to take them back to where they had been two months ago.

Because she had never forgotten how amazing that night had been. How Linc had made her feel like the most beautiful woman in the world, just by the way he'd taken the time to kiss her body, lingering with his touch, his mouth, over every inch, before finally bringing her complete satisfaction.

"I don't know," she whispered, dipping her head into the curve of his neck, trying to quell the fire in her veins, the furious beating of her heart. Trying like heck to find some sort of a coherent thought.

What was she doing? This wasn't where she wanted to go. What she had intended to do.

But, oh…for just a moment, she wanted this and more.

She'd come to Vegas, fully intending to return to San Diego alone. And yet every minute she spent with Lincoln Curtis she got more and more wrapped up in him, even though she knew—

The minute she told him she was carrying his baby— that he was about to become a father—he would turn his back on her as surely as her ex-husband had. Hadn't he already made that clear, over and over again?

Linc did not want children of his own. And he surely wasn't going to want this one.

The baby. The baby comes first.

The reality slapped her out of the muddled fog of desire. "I'm sorry," she said. "I...I can't do this." Molly slipped out of Linc's arms and drifted away from him, heading for the boat. She hoisted herself onto the platform, then stood, letting the sun warm her skin as the water dripped off. In a second, Linc was behind her.

"What is it? Did I say something wrong?"

"No. I just...I remembered I have someplace to be." She wasn't any better at lying than she was at sticking to her original intentions. She turned away so he wouldn't see the deception written all over her face, and climbed back into the boat.

Linc followed, picking up a towel to mop at his face and arms. "Someplace you have to be? Now?"

She nodded, keeping her face averted by using her towel to dry her hair, and making sure to keep the long beach towel hanging over the front of her as she did so. She should have thought before she bought a two-piece swimsuit that the style would expose her stomach to his gaze.

She'd noticed him staring at her. Had he seen that she'd put on some weight? Noticed the slight bulge in her belly? If he had, he hadn't asked. "I have a couple of friends in Vegas and I completely forgot I agreed to meet one of them for an early dinner. I'm sorry, but we need to cut this short."

He considered her for a long moment, as if trying to decide whether to confront her on her story, then finally let it go. She thought she saw a flicker of disappointment in his features. "I suppose that's just as well," he said, his voice colder than the water had been. Whatever might have happened between them was over now. She'd accomplished her goal—alienating Linc. She drew no satisfaction from winning that battle.

"I really should get back to the office," he continued. "They've probably sent out a search party for me by now."

"Back to reality, huh?"

"Always. I might be able to escape for a minute, but in the end…" Linc paused to look out over the calm waters of Lake Mead for a moment before returning his gaze to her. "I'm still the boss and that means my priority is always the business first—"

"And a personal life second," she finished, recalling what he'd said to Harry in the aquarium.

A lesson she'd do well to remember.

For her sake, and the baby's.

CHAPTER NINE

MOLLY curved into Linc's arms, pressed against his warm chest, satisfied and happier than she could ever remember feeling. He pressed a kiss to the top of her head, then slid a hand down her back, the message clear.

He wanted her. Again.

She smiled, thrilled and flattered. Who could have known that this man—a stranger—could awaken such incredible feelings inside her? That someone she didn't even know could make her feel so beautiful, so desired? Could erase the years of doubt implanted by Doug, who had made her feel like she wasn't enough. Not perfect enough, not right for his rigid life.

That her desire for more, for a marriage that fulfilled her needs, too, was ridiculous.

Linc tipped her chin to meet his and kissed her, long, hard, with no doubt about what was to come next. More of the same long, leisurely passionate lovemaking they had already enjoyed. They hadn't slept a wink that night—and she didn't care.

She wanted only to enjoy him, to enjoy this exquisite feeling again and again and—

Ringing. Something was ringing. What on earth?

Molly awoke with a start, and sat up, disoriented at first. Where was she? Not in the bed at the Bellagio, which was what she'd been dreaming. Not in her bed at home in San Diego.

Oh, goodness. She'd fallen asleep on the desk in the Research and Development room. It had to be the result of the long day in the sun, coupled with the pregnancy—making her tired and sending her hormones into overdrive.

Causing that extremely vivid dream.

The ringing continued, and Molly looked around, confused for a second longer before she realized it was coming from her computer. Jayne! She'd forgotten to call Jayne on the video phone. The two of them had been chatting almost daily, conversations Molly looked forward to because they kept her connected not just with her friend, but with her life back home. She clicked on the video chat software, answered the call, and loaded the Web cam, straightening her hair as she did, and hoping like heck she'd erased all visual traces of that sexy, detailed dream.

Of Linc.

Jayne's face filled the screen. "Hey, Jayne, nice to see you!" Molly said.

"You, too! How you feeling?"

"Fine. A little tired." A few days ago she'd told Jayne about the baby on the way. Like Alex and Serena, Jayne had been overjoyed, yet worried about her friend.

Molly sat back in the chair in the R & D office, glad Roy had already gone home for the day and she had the room to herself. Right now, all she wanted was to be alone. It had been two hours since she'd returned from Lake Mead, and she'd done nothing but try to avoid Linc.

She'd lied about having to meet a friend. Lied about

needing to get out of there. Lied because he'd gotten too close, and she didn't know what to do about it.

"How are things with the baby's father?" Jayne asked, her movement slightly slowed and exaggerated because of the video conference connection between Molly's computer at Curtis Systems and her desktop back in San Diego, where Jayne sat with Rocky on her lap.

Molly sighed. She toyed with the baby journal beside her, still just as blank as ever. "Complicated."

Had Molly really thought she could work for Linc—the man she had spent one incredible night with—and not be reminded of the time she'd spent in his arms? Had she really thought being his employee would allow her to gain access to his personal life? That he'd just open up to her, as if she were his best friend?

She should have done this differently. Just told him straight out that she was pregnant and seen what happened from there.

"Does he know about the baby yet?" Jayne asked. Rocky's ears perked up.

Molly shook her head. "I haven't found a way to tell him yet."

"Moll, you have to. You can't just let something like that wait. I mean, he's going to figure it out in a few months anyway."

"I know, but…" She let out another long breath. "I'm afraid of what he'll do when I tell him."

Jayne laughed. "What, something really terrible, like marry you?"

"Yeah." She could see that in Linc. The overwhelming urge to do the honorable thing. Except that would put her right back where she'd already been before—married to a man who was her complete opposite. A man who'd only married her because it was the right thing to do, not because he loved her, or because he wanted to form a family with her. She and Linc may have shared an attraction, okay, an amazingly hot attraction, but clearly they wanted different things for their futures and their lives.

She wanted the kind of happy marriage her parents had had for thirty-plus years. They had been in love, and it had shown in every gesture, every word. That was what Molly wanted, not a business partnership, which was the kind of thing she could see Linc proposing.

"Or worse," Molly continued, "he could not want the baby."

"You'll never know if you don't talk to him."

Molly drummed her fingers on the desk. She knew that. And yet she kept putting off telling Linc the truth. At some point, she had to tell him. He deserved to know. It was the right thing to do—for him and for the baby. And if after she told him he wanted nothing to do with her or the baby, then that was his loss.

She would have at least done the right thing.

And she was okay with that, she really was. At least, that was what she told herself.

"I know. I just need some time." She put the baby journal into her tote bag, then set the bag on the floor and forced the thoughts of Linc out of her mind. She had done enough thinking about him for one day. Definitely enough, especially after that dream. "So tell me, how are things in San Diego? Are you taking good care of my garden? How's Rocky?"

"Garden is, umm...okay," Jayne said. "I'm no green thumb, but nothing has died yet." The two women laughed. "Rocky's fine. Missing you, I'm sure, because he sits at the door every day, waiting. I think he thinks you're going to walk through that door at any minute."

Molly laughed. "Hey, Rock, I'll be back soon. I promise. Ask Auntie Jayne to give you extra treats." Rocky woofed.

Jayne scratched behind the Jack Russell's ears. He let out a satisfied groan and settled against Jayne's chest. "Oh, hey, I almost forgot to tell you. An invitation came in the mail for you. Do you want me to open it? In case it's something important you might need to come home for?"

"Sure." Molly watched as Jayne held up a thick peach envelope. She heard the sounds of the paper tearing, a card being withdrawn.

Then Jayne gasping. "Uh, Molly, I'll just throw this away."

"What? What is it?"

"You…you don't want to know."

"No, seriously, go ahead. Tell me."

Jayne hesitated, then turned the card to face the computer screen. It took Molly a second to process the image, and when she did—

Her stomach clenched. She couldn't believe it. He wouldn't. He hadn't.

But the proof was there, in a blissful black-and-white photograph.

Dr. Douglas Wyndham was marrying a woman named Lisa Jenkins in two weeks. That news didn't hit Molly as hard as what else she saw. In Lisa's arms—

A brand-new baby boy.

Jayne lowered the picture, and sent Molly a sympathetic smile. "He's a jerk, you know that, don't you? One, for inviting you, and two, for leaving you. If there's a king of jerks, it's him."

"I can't believe…" Molly shook her head. "He said he never wanted children."

"Maybe he still doesn't. Molly, you're better off without him."

"Oh, I agree." And as she said that, she knew she was over her ex-husband, and though the thoughtlessness of his inviting her to his wedding hurt, she had no second thoughts about divorcing him. "I just never expected him, of all people, to change his mind." The invitation, and the image of Doug with a baby, stung. All those dreams she'd had for so long, crushed in a marriage that had suffocated her—and now he'd gone and created that with someone else.

And here she sat, finally having the baby she'd always dreamed of—

Alone.

If only Linc was—

Well, he wasn't. Once again, she'd chosen badly.

Hadn't Linc made it clear at least a half a dozen times in the conversations they'd had that he wasn't interested in children? That he had no time in his life for a family? That his priorities always—always—came back to work?

No matter how much Molly might wish the image on that card was of Linc, herself and their baby, that wasn't to be. And the sooner she accepted it, the sooner she could move forward.

Alone.

Tears stung at the back of Molly's eyes, but she refused to let them fall. Instead, she changed the subject, asking Jayne about her job. For the next thirty minutes she and Jayne shared a chatty conversation, the kind only good friends could have, about nothing and everything. Jayne talked to her about where the baby's crib would go, what color she was thinking of painting the baby's room, all happy, future plans. By the time Molly was ready to disconnect from the videophone she felt much better about the entire situation. She should have known her friends would understand. They'd be there to support her, no matter what.

"I gotta get going, but promise me you're going to tell him."

"I will," Molly said.

"And no matter what," Jayne said. "You know me, Alex and Serena are always here if you want to talk. Or shop for baby clothes."

Molly laughed, then said goodbye to Jayne. After she hung up, she placed a hand on her abdomen. Inside, a life grew, too small to see yet, but soon it would announce itself. "Hey, baby," she whispered, and as she did a thread of connection seemed to grow between herself and the tiny person she had yet to meet. "Soon, I'm going to tell your daddy all about you. And I hope he's as happy to hear you're on the way as I am."

Linc managed two hours of work. With Herculean effort.

The entire time his mind kept replaying the day with Molly. From the minute she'd "kidnapped" him to the second she'd said goodbye in front of the office as soon as the town car slowed to a stop. She hadn't, as he'd expected, headed to the right when she entered the building, which would have led to the parking garage and her rental car.

No, instead he'd seen her disappear into the recesses of the building, and suspected she'd gone over to R & D to work. To avoid him, he was sure.

The question was why. Why she'd lied, and why she had cut their day short.

A day that had been, in his mind, perfect. When she'd first proposed the idea of ditching work and running off to Lake Mead, he'd thought she was crazy. Thought the guilt about leaving his desk for so many hours would eat him alive.

It hadn't. Instead, he'd returned to his office refreshed, recharged, and except for being completely distracted by the mental image of Molly in a bikini, and ongoing thoughts of kissing her, he'd been ready to get back to work. Maybe Molly was right. Maybe he could afford a day off here and there.

Then his gaze strayed to the photo on the corner of his desk. Marcus, with his wife, his two children. Guilt slammed into Linc all over again, and he decided no. His job was here, providing for the fatherless children of his brother.

Keeping his promise.

Not getting involved with a woman who personified two-point-five kids and a house in the suburbs.

Yeah, if that was so, then why did his mind keep going back again and again to the memory of her in his arms in the water? To how wonderful it felt to touch her again? To kiss her?

Conner popped his head into Linc's office. "Hey, Linc, you still here? I thought you took the day off."

"I did, but I came back. You know me. Can't stay away from this place." Linc let out a laugh, but it scraped past his throat.

"Figured that." Conner held up a folder. "I have next year's budget projections for you. I was going to leave them on your desk, but since you're here, do you have a few minutes before the meeting at five?"

Another meeting. Another round of facts and figures. On any other day Linc wouldn't care. He'd simply move from task to task, checking them off on his list with satisfaction. Today, despite feeling energized by the half day off, he couldn't have cared less if he accomplished one thing or twenty. Because, no matter how much he tried to convince himself otherwise, there was one detail that he had left unsettled, and until he had that cleared up, he knew his concentration was going to be shot to hell.

Conner entered Linc's office, clearly expecting Linc to say yes, and started to hand the folder to his boss. Linc put out his hand—and pushed the folder back. Working was pointless, at least for now. He hadn't accomplished half of what he normally did in the last two hours and he sure as hell wasn't going to do much better in the next two.

"You know, I think I'm going to leave early today," Linc said. "I have some other…unfinished business to attend to first. Let's reschedule the meeting for tomorrow. Let everyone go home, have dinner with their families, rather than try to cram one more meeting into the day."

Conner's jaw dropped. "Leave early? I didn't think those two words were in your vocabulary."

"They're not." Linc grinned. "I just have something… else I want to do tonight. Trust me, I'm not changing into a slacker. Tomorrow will run like normal."

"Oh, I always have hope you'll change, at least a little. I'm an optimist, always an optimist." Conner shot him a smile, then backed out of the office. "I'll reschedule. And let you get out of here. Hopefully to do something fun."

As soon as Conner was gone, Linc shut down his computer and headed down in the elevator. He reached for the lobby button, hovered over the *L*, then pressed the number six instead.

On the sixth floor, he headed for the R & D room. Chances were, Molly wasn't even here. That she had indeed gone out to dinner with her friend, that he'd been wrong about her going back to work. But he couldn't leave without knowing for sure.

Without asking her why she had left so abruptly.

But, no, the door was open. He saw Molly gathering her things, about to leave. He could easily walk away, let the day end as it had. Or not.

"Molly."

She turned at the sound of his voice, surprised, and the tote bag in her hands slipped to the floor, spilling its contents. She bent quickly to gather them up again, but not before he saw the book that landed on top. Linc bent down, picked it up—

And froze.

A hardcover Memories for Your Baby journal.

A baby journal? Why would she have something like that? Maybe it was a gift for a friend?

Molly snatched it out of his hand and shoved the book into her bag. "Uh, thank you."

He thought about today. About her going green at the sight of the bait. At the little bit of extra weight around her waist. And now the book. Most of all he thought of that night—that crazy, intoxicating night when both of them had been acting too fast, too rashly—

"Are you pregnant?" he said, the words blurting out of him before he could think of a better way to ask the question.

"I…" Her eyes widened, and a flush filled her cheeks.

That was answer enough for him. "When were you going to tell me?"

"Soon, I swear. I just…I couldn't find the right time."

"Is it…mine?"

She recoiled, as if he'd slapped her, and he wanted to take the question back. "Of course. You think I run around having one-night stands with strangers all the time?"

"I didn't mean that, Molly. At all. I meant that…well, you could have been in a relationship when we met. It's not like we talked about a lot of those kinds of things."

She busied herself with picking up the rest of the books. He bent to help her, and his hand brushed against hers. She jerked away. "I haven't been in a relationship or with any-one in…a long time."

"Oh." That meant only one thing. The child was his.

Linc turned away and ran a hand through his hair. "This was a complication I wasn't planning on."

She snorted. "It's a baby, Linc. Not a complication."

"I'm not prepared to have a family. In fact, it's not in my plans at all."

He saw the disappointment that shimmered in her eyes, the way her face fell, and the distance she put between them in two steps. But what was he supposed to do? Lie? Or tell her the truth—that for just a split second there he'd imagined having it all? That he'd looked at her belly and thought of what it would be like to hold his newborn son or daughter?

Then he'd remembered that he, of all people, shouldn't be a parent. He'd been a terrible older brother. What made him think he could be any kind of parent?

"I'm not asking you to do anything at all," Molly said.

"But there are certain things I should do," Linc said. "As the father."

"Such as?"

His mind went to the first, most obvious need, and he reached into the breast pocket of his suit to withdraw a leather checkbook and a pen. "You'll need money for the child. For diapers and cribs and—"

"Are you paying me off?" The shock in her voice raised the words by several decibels.

"Not at all. I'm merely giving you money—"

"To get rid of the problem. The 'complication.'" She threw air quotes around the word, nearly spitting it back into his face. Molly shook her head, then headed for the door. "I thought I knew you, Linc, I really did. But I was wrong."

Before he could stop her, she was gone. The door slammed behind her, leaving no doubt about Molly's feelings. She wanted nothing to do with Linc. Did he blame her, really? He couldn't have handled that worse if he tried.

Damn.

He'd turned to leave when he noticed something parked against the leg of the desk. Molly's tote bag. As he picked up the bag, the book resting atop the others inside toppled out of the tote and fell to the floor. The Memories for Your Baby journal. Linc began to flip through it.

It was one of those books you filled in, the kind that asked questions, and the parents-to-be supplied the answers. A few pages in, he found one labeled "ABOUT YOUR DADDY."

FATHER'S NAME: *Lincoln Curtis*
BIRTHDAY: *??*
EYE COLOR: *Blue*
HAIR COLOR: *Dark Brown*
OCCUPATION: *CEO*
WHERE WE MET: *Over a glass of wine in Las Vegas*

His mind rocketed back to that night in the Bellagio, to the frenzied passion between the two of them, their rush to get upstairs to a room, and the first time they'd made love—

Without taking precautions first.

Stupid, he'd known, but then, the next time, when his mind had been clearer and he'd taken his time making love to Molly, he'd been smart. Thinking, like an idiot who hadn't taken Health class in fifth grade, just one time wasn't enough to get anyone pregnant.

Linc turned every page in the journal, and found nothing but blank pages for things like "Where Your Father Grew Up." "His Happiest Childhood Memory." "Names He Wanted for You."

Deep in the book he found a few lines filled in, with information clearly gleaned from the conversation with Harry at the aquarium. However, the questions she'd asked him over the last few days suddenly made sense. And the blank pages were testament to how little he had opened up to her.

He hadn't opened his heart at all. Merely his checkbook.

Linc let out a long sigh and put the tote bag back where he had found it. But he took the journal with him, turned off the light and left the room.

CHAPTER TEN

MOLLY woke up before the sun. Her morning sickness had begun to abate, and after a few crackers and a little ginger ale she felt fine—at least from the pregnancy nausea. But from her emotions—

Not so good.

What had she expected Linc to do when he found out about the baby? Open his arms, welcome her into his embrace and propose some version of the three of them living happily ever after?

Well...

Yes. Part of her, deep down inside, had hoped for that, as insane as it sounded. Even the side of her that was realistic and cautious had not expected him to throw money at her, like she was a problem he could buy his way out of.

She drew herself up, refusing to give in to the turmoil of emotions churning inside her. She was fine, just fine, she told herself, and that was what she was going to tell Linc, too. So he hadn't leaped for joy, exploded with a smile or danced around the room with her.

That was to be expected. She had, after all, kept this a secret, and probably shouldn't have. She refused to acknowledge the disappointment about his reaction settling inside her.

Molly thought of her own father, of how he'd been there to teach her to ride a bike, to build a birdhouse, to shoot a basketball. She wanted her child to have the same things. Surely Linc did, too?

She would talk to him. Maybe he'd been shocked, and that explained his reaction.

She got dressed, then left her apartment. In the elevator, instead of pressing the button for lobby, she hit the *P* for penthouse. In her mind, she composed a thousand different things she wanted to say to him, but as soon as he opened the door she went mute.

Linc stood in his spacious apartment, shirtless, wearing only dark blue dress pants. He had a defined, well-built body, muscular, with a firm six-pack and a solid strength that seemed to beg a woman to step into his arms and rely on him. Despite her best intentions, desire coursed through Molly's veins, and her mind went back to the day before, to being in the water and pressed against Linc's warm, solid chest. The vivid dream she'd had yesterday had done nothing but compound those feelings, and remind her all over again how good being with him could be.

God, she wanted him.

Even if having him was all wrong for her. And he had made it clear he wanted the complete opposite of what she did.

Focus, Molly. Focus.

"Molly." Surprise lit his features. "What are you doing here so early?"

"I wanted to talk to you. Alone."

Linc stepped back and gestured her into the apartment. As soon as she entered Linc's personal space, she was struck by how—

How un-Linc it was.

She'd expected an apartment as stark and linear as the cor-

SHIRLEY JUMP   147

porate offices of Curtis Systems. Instead, she found a warm, cozy and inviting place filled with overstuffed caramel leather furniture, deep, plush, off-white rugs, and pictures—

Tons and tons of pictures. Frames of all shapes, sizes and styles dominated the sofa table, the shelves on either side of the fireplace, the long windowsill against the far wall.

"Your apartment is...wonderful," she said, turning a slow circle, taking in the cook's kitchen, the intimate dining room, the comfortable living room. He had an eclectic mix of furniture, from the antique cherry buffet table to the more modern leather furniture. Yet somehow it all seemed to flow in a happy marriage of style. "Not at all what I thought it would look like."

"Thank you. A lot of the pieces I inherited when my parents passed away ten years ago," he said. "But I have to admit I hired a decorator to put it all together. My talents don't extend very far past the boardroom."

She shot him a smile. "Oh, I don't know about that."

And just like that, she was flirting with him again. Every time she turned around, she got sidetracked, derailed by her hormones. That was what it had to be—the overload of estrogen from the pregnancy.

Not the fact that a muscular, sexy Lincoln Curtis was standing less than a foot away from her. Bare-chested. Tempting.

And sending her mind right back to that dream she'd had yesterday. To the memory of his chest against hers in the water, that sensuous slippery feeling of skin on skin. Of kissing him—oh, kissing him.

Yeah, right. Not that at all.

"Coffee?"

"Huh?" She had to drag her gaze away from his chest and focus again. He'd asked her a question.

"Would you like some coffee?" Linc asked her.

"No, thank you." She trailed a hand along the back of the leather sofa. She couldn't stand here all day admiring his apartment. She had come here for a reason and she needed to get to it.

"Why did you connect with me that night in the bar?" she asked. "There are thousands of single women in Vegas on any given night. Why me?"

Why an ordinary kindergarten teacher from San Diego, when a man like Lincoln Curtis could have his choice of anyone?

He gestured toward the balcony, and to two wide wicker seats placed beneath an awning that provided welcome shade from the Vegas sun. They went outside, and settled into the comfortable furniture. "That answer's simple. Because you weren't then, and still aren't, like any of the women I've ever met in Vegas. Not that I meet very many."

The compliment warmed her. "What do you mean?"

He let out a long breath. "I don't date a lot, as I'm sure you've realized, just based on my work schedule. And when I do meet women, most of them see me as..." He paused a moment. "As Lincoln Curtis, not Linc."

"You mean as the CEO, not as the man." She could see why. In a suit, and in his element at work, Linc cut an imposing figure. She hadn't heard a single employee of Curtis Systems call him anything other than Mr. Curtis. She was sure no one could imagine him as anything else, picture him in a different setting than the corporate one.

"When I went into the bar that night, I purposely dressed down," he said. "I didn't want to be seen as a boss, or heck, even a businessman. I just wanted, for once, to be... me."

She smiled. "I know the feeling."

"How so?"

She let out a long sigh. If she wanted Linc to open up to her, then perhaps she needed to do a little opening up of her own. "I used to be married to a doctor. It didn't last long and we got divorced two years ago. He was...very structured. Kept our lives in this tight little line. I didn't realize how much that suffocated me until after I got divorced. It was like I took off the ring and suddenly became me again." She'd later seen how she had lost herself in her marriage to Doug, and once they were apart she'd gone back to feeling happy. Free. Living a life that didn't have every moment planned.

"I can't imagine you married to someone like that," Linc said.

"In the beginning, he was charming. I guess with the right smile you end up overlooking a lot of faults." She shook her head. "Anyway, it's over. And I'm not going to make that mistake again."

Linc met her gaze, and she wondered if he knew that she meant she had no intentions of falling for him, regardless of those kisses yesterday. She didn't want Lincoln Curtis, CEO. She wanted Linc, the man she'd met that night, the man she'd seen at Lake Mead and on the boat—

But he never seemed to stay around. Especially not yesterday. Disappointment filled her again.

"I know what you mean. I almost got married myself."

"You did?"

He nodded. "But I couldn't be the right kind of husband, so I broke things off. She deserved more than I could give."

Molly wondered what he meant by that. What kind of husband he couldn't be. Was it just then, or now, too?

"When I met you," Linc went on, "it was like stepping into another world. Our conversation was so...ordinary. So normal. You didn't start out with the sound-bite line."

"Sound-bite line?"

"You know, when you hear someone interviewed on TV? The first few words out of any reporter's mouth are the person's name, age, occupation. A lot of the women I've met in the past have only been interested in that. Maybe they want to make sure I'm employed or have enough to cover the dinner bill."

He let out a sharp laugh that spoke of a long line of disappointing dates. A wave of sympathy ran through Molly.

"But you…" His voice trailed off.

She dipped her head, remembering her opening line, spurred by the activities at the table across from them. Almost embarrassed by its simplicity. "I asked you about your most memorable birthday."

"It was so…unexpected. So different." He smiled. "And when I told you—"

"About your seventh birthday," she finished, the memory still vivid, as clear today as it had been that night. Wishing she'd come up with something more clever. "When you got your first two-wheeler bike."

"And my first broken bone." Linc chuckled. "It was quite the ice-breaker."

She shrugged, as if it was nothing. "That's just something I use with my classes to help the kids get to know each other."

His gaze met hers. "It works."

She bit her lip, and asked the other big question that had bothered her ever since she'd arrived in Vegas. "And was the man I met that night, the dressed-down one, was he the real Linc?"

The one who could live an ordinary life, with a wife and a child? She left those words unspoken, because she didn't want to see that damned checkbook again and have her heart broken twice in two days.

Linc's gaze went to the desert, and he stared at it for so long Molly thought he wasn't going to answer her. "It doesn't matter if he was or he wasn't. I can't be that man, even if I wanted to be."

Frustration bubbled up inside of her. "What does that mean? You can't live an ordinary life?"

He turned back to her. "I shouldn't. I'd be no good at it."

Molly sighed. What had she been expecting? That just because she asked the question, Linc would supply the answer she wanted?

"I…I should go," she said, getting to her feet. "I don't want to make you late."

And I don't want to cry in front of you. Don't want to let you know how much I wanted to hear you say something else. Wanted to hear you say you'd been wrong yesterday. You changed your mind.

She had made it to the French doors and almost stepped back inside before he spoke.

"It's not that I don't want what everyone else has, Molly. Or want to be a father, especially to my own child. It's that I can't."

Molly froze and turned back to him. "That's insane. All you have to do is try, Linc."

"I have. And I was awful at it." He sighed. "I let down the one person I was supposed to protect."

She couldn't imagine powerful, dedicated Linc doing any such thing. "Who?"

He had turned back to the desert, and was silent for so long Molly was sure he wasn't going to answer her. She stepped back out onto the patio and came up behind Linc, laying a hand on his shoulder. "Who?" she asked again.

"My brother." The words slipped out softly.

"Marcus."

He nodded, then let out a breath. "I made a promise to take care of him. To be there for him. And I broke that." Linc pivoted toward Molly, and in his eyes she saw pain, grief, regret. "I wasn't there for him when he needed me, and that's why I can't promise to be there for anyone else."

"Linc—"

"No, Molly, don't." He put up a hand. "If you need money, you need a house, car, anything else, I'll provide it. But don't ask me to be a part of raising this child."

Hurt and disappointment coursed through her. She should have known better than to come here, to try and change his mind. Hadn't he made it clear from the beginning that he wasn't the family man type? "I only came to Vegas to get to know you, in case the baby had questions. Just enough information to fill a few pages of that book, and then…" She forced herself to keep going, to push the words past that stubborn lump of despair that refused to go away. "I'll go back to San Diego and raise the baby myself. I don't expect you to marry me or be any more involved than that."

"You don't want me to be a part of the baby's life? Or yours?"

"I don't *expect* you to be," she repeated, because expecting and wanting were two different things, and if she admitted that deep down inside she had hoped he'd want to be part of their lives, she would cry. "You've made yourself very clear."

Her mind, her silly mind, couldn't seem to let go of that Christmas card image. Of her, Linc, the baby in front of a Christmas tree, all smiles and hope.

Ridiculous. Why couldn't she get over that and face reality?

"I'm not trying to hurt you, Molly, believe me."

"It's not me you're hurting. It's you, and our baby. Like it or not, this baby will be here in seven months. And you're going to be missing something pretty spectacular when it arrives." She turned away, then took a step back. "You know, the man I met two months ago was the kind of man I could have—" She cut off the sentence. She refused to be vulnerable. Refused to fall into that trap again. Hadn't she learned her lesson with Doug? Sharing her dreams had done nothing but get them rejected. "The kind of man who could have taken a risk like this. Who wouldn't have let fear hold him back from one of the best gifts life has to offer."

He let out a sigh. "You know I'll do right by you and this child. You don't have to worry about that."

She shook her head. "I don't want your *money*, Linc. This was never about money."

"I can't settle down in the suburbs in the little picket fence house. I'm not that kind of man."

"One of these days, this baby—our child, *your* child— is going to grow up and ask me…" She inhaled, because the next words hurt even before they left her throat. "Where's my daddy? Why isn't he here? Didn't he want me? What do you want me to tell him or her?"

Linc turned around, placing his back against the railing. "The truth. That a man like me has no business raising a child. I'm good at being a CEO, Molly. But when it comes to people—"

He cut off the words, and she waited for him to finish.

"With people, I'm just not the one you want to pin all your hopes on."

Molly's spirits deflated. Whether she'd consciously thought it or not, she had been hoping. For Linc to find out about the baby and change his mind, for him to come around and somehow be as excited as she was.

For him to not be like her ex-husband.

"I'll be sure to send you pictures every once in a while," she said, forcing herself not to cry. To hold it together until she got out of this apartment. Got away from him. "That way, at least you'll know what your child looks like. That we're okay. But I won't… I don't expect anything else."

Then Molly left, her heart breaking as she finally realized that the Linc she had met had been a temporary figure, like a ghost. While the real one wasn't the man she wanted.

At all.

Linc stayed on his balcony for a long time after Molly left. Then he wandered his apartment, tracing his life through the photos that lined nearly every surface of his rooms.

When he finally went to work, and took his place behind the mahogany desk that had been his nearly since the day Curtis Systems had opened its doors, he didn't last long.

He buzzed down to his driver. "Bring the car around please, Saul. I've got someone I have to see."

The software program had come together in record speed. Jerome had only been needed for the first few days because Roy had an uncanny ability for transforming Molly's ideas into computer code, and by the middle of the afternoon the two of them had finished the rough program, and Molly was confident it captured Linc's original vision.

"Looks great," she said. "I think kids are going to love it."

"Next week, we'll do some testing, work out some of the bugs in this basic version," Roy said. "Then we can work on documentation, and take the beta version to the brainiacs up in Marketing. See what they think, make any necessary tweaks—"

"You'll do that," Molly said, the decision finalizing in

her mind as the words left her. Really, did she have any other choice? After this morning, she didn't see another reason to stay in Vegas. Linc had made his feelings clear. "I have to go back to San Diego."

Roy stared at her. "San Diego? Why?"

"This was always a temporary job. By day I'm a kindergarten teacher." She tried to smile, but the gesture fell flat. "I just don't think this job will work out."

"But...but you were fabulous at it."

"You were," she said, pointing at the computer. "You're the one who created the program."

Roy laughed. "Molly, I write code. I'm like the mechanic who puts together the engine for the car. The engine needs the hot, sexy car design to make it sell to consumers. That's where you came in. You provided all the ideas for the design. I'm just the geek who translated them into computer language."

The flattery warmed Molly. All these years, she'd worked as a teacher, and although she had enjoyed her job a great deal, she had never done anything she could point to and say it was hers—her idea, her execution. If this program became a reality, and thousands of children ended up playing Inside Out Games, and even better learning, then she would know she had a part in that. How amazing would it be to see a child playing the game, and know she had had a part in creating it?

That realization brought a new kind of job satisfaction that she had never felt before. She'd never imagined she could have another career—and, even more, enjoy it so much.

Too bad she was going to have to say goodbye before she barely got started. She glanced at the computer, and a sense of loss washed over her. Maybe someday she'd see the program in stores, or in the school where she worked. That would be good enough. It would have to be.

She couldn't keep on working here, seeing Linc every day, knowing how he felt.

Knowing he didn't want the same things as her. The life she wanted.

Even more, their child.

"Thanks, Roy. Really." She rose, and gathered her tote bag and her purse. "I enjoyed working with you."

"You're really leaving us?"

She nodded.

"What about Mr. Curtis?"

"He'll find someone else. There are plenty of people who can do my job."

Roy leaned back, draping an arm over his chair. "I'm probably way out of line for saying this, but I've worked here six years, and I know Mr. Curtis about as well as anyone. He's been…different since you came to work here. Happier. I mean, that whole thing about taking the day off? I have no idea how you talked him into it. He never does that. The rest of us who work for him, we think he puts in way too many hours, takes too much on his shoulders. But you know, that's Mr. Curtis."

"Yeah, I know," she said. Too well.

"I'm not trying to tell you what to do, but if there's any chance you can stay here instead of going back to San Diego…" Roy shrugged again. "Well, it'd sure be nice to see the boss smiling like he has been the last few days."

Molly nodded, but made no promises. She couldn't. She and Linc were over, and that was the way it had to stay. She couldn't stay here and keep on hoping for an impossible situation to change. It would break her heart and, when her child was old enough to understand, break his or her heart, too. She couldn't stand by and watch that happen.

The reality was the same now as it had been this morning. She was going home—to raise her child alone.

So she said goodbye to Roy and left the room.

She slipped into the elevator, grateful to find it empty for once. She leaned against the wall, and now, finally, let the tears fall. In a few hours she'd be back in San Diego. Back in her cozy little bungalow.

Leaving Lincoln Curtis far behind in Las Vegas.

For the second time.

CHAPTER ELEVEN

Linc sat on the low-slung white sofa, thinking he'd waited too damned long to come here. He'd let too much time pass—

Because it was easier that way.

"Here you go." Renee Curtis laid a glass of lemonade in front of him, then sat in a matching armchair on the other side of the glass-and-chrome coffee table. "The kids will be home soon. They're next door at my neighbor Jeannie's house, swimming in her pool." She laughed a little. "Doesn't matter how nice our pool is, the one in the next yard is always more fun."

"How are the kids?"

Renee glanced out the window, at the white Colonial a few hundred yards away. "They're okay. It gets both harder and easier as time goes by. If that makes any sense."

Linc sipped at the lemonade, not out of thirst, but out of something to do. In the three years since his brother had died, he'd tried very hard not to have these conversations with his sister-in-law. He'd sent checks. Birthday cards. Christmas presents. But not himself, not any more than necessary. It wasn't that he didn't love or care about Marcus's widow and two children, it was that seeing them was too painful. Avoiding them was easier all around, for both sides.

"How does it get easier?" he asked Renee, because he sure as hell wanted to know the answer to that question. He hadn't found it, not in three years.

She sighed. "The kids get used to not having him here. They move forward. After a while, you get to the point where you stop thinking about it every five minutes. Then that makes it harder, because when you do stop, and realize he's gone—" She inhaled. "It hurts all over again."

Guilt roared through him at the pain lining her face. "I'm sorry, Renee," Linc said, thinking he couldn't say the words enough times. "I'm so sorry."

A sad smile curved across her face. "Linc, you don't have to—"

"I should have been there that day." He let out a breath, then rose and faced the same window Renee had just been looking out of. He could see the corner of the neighbor's pool, and the ripples of bright blue water, but not his niece and nephew. Through the glass, though, he could hear their happy shouts, and knew they were doing okay. He was grateful for that. "If I had never left, he would have taken care of himself, taken the medication—"

"Linc, he was a grown man. He made his choices."

"I was the one who was supposed to watch out for him. I promised them. I promised—" His voice broke on the last few words, and he gripped the window frame, the outside images blurring.

"It wasn't your fault, Linc."

Linc shook his head. He knew the truth. Marcus had been his responsibility, and, as smart as his brother was, he hadn't been smart when it came to his health. "He told me not to worry, that he'd take his medication. But I should have known better. He was always forgetting, and because I wasn't there—"

"You couldn't police him every minute of the day. He was an adult. He didn't even—" Renee cut off her sentence, and in the short syllables Linc heard the same echo of regret that was arcing through his own chest. "He never even told me."

Linc turned to his sister-in-law, and put a hand on her arm. "He didn't want you to worry."

A bittersweet smile crested on her lips. "What kind of husband doesn't tell his own wife he has a heart condition?"

"One who didn't want you to see him as weak. Marcus hated being sick. Hated everything to do with being what he saw, I guess, as something less than normal. He never told anyone."

"I wish he had." Tears glimmered in her eyes. "It should never have been just your responsibility, Linc."

He turned away from the forgiveness in her face, in her tone. Renee had never blamed him, but Linc had done enough blaming for a dozen people. "If I had—"

"If you had done A or B, he still could have had a heart attack." Renee came up behind him and put a hand on his shoulder. "Marcus loved his job, Linc. He loved his life. He was all about having a good time with whatever time he had."

Linc nodded, mute. His devil-may-care brother who had lived for the moment, in the moment.

"It wasn't work that caused his heart to fail. It was just…his time. You, of all people, should know that. The doctor said—"

Linc wheeled around. "I don't care what the doctor said, Renee. If I had been here, I would have made sure he took every last pill. Gone to the doctor when he started feeling bad, instead of going on about his day like nothing was wrong. That was *my job*, to watch over Marcus, protect him. The only one I failed at."

Renee put a hand on Linc's face and shook her head. "No, Linc, you didn't. And you know darn well that Marcus would tell you the same thing if he was here. Why do you keep beating yourself up over something you can't change?"

A door opened in the back of the house and giggles and shouts exploded inside the room. "Mom! Can we get a slide on our pool, too?" The voice was followed a second later by the twin images of Marcus—

Anna and Daniel. The two children slid to a stop. Anna, the younger of the two, tipped her head in confusion, but Daniel's face broke into a grin. "Hi, Uncle Linc."

"Hello, Daniel. Anna." Linc couldn't believe how much eight-year-old Daniel looked like his father. He had the same lopsided smile, the same wide blue eyes, the same cowlick that made his hair curve across the front of his head. "I brought you two a few things." Linc turned and handed each of the kids a bag filled with a few toys he'd picked up on his way to the house. He'd had no idea what to buy, and simply trusted the salesclerk in the toy store.

Daniel exclaimed over the remote control car, and fair-haired, blue-eyed Anna clutched the baby doll to her chest, telling Linc he'd done all right for a guy who knew nothing about kids.

For a second, his mind wandered to Molly. To the child she carried. He saw his own image in the faces of his niece and nephew and wondered what it would be like to see that smile someday on his own child's face. To buy something and know he'd gotten it right. Picked out just the right toy truck or perfect stuffed animal. Then have his child run up to him, arms out, a hug ready—

Linc pushed the image aside. He'd made his choices. The best ones for him, and for Molly.

Marcus's children thanked him, then headed back outside to play with their new gifts.

"Thanks, Linc," Renee said.

"Least I can do," he said, tearing his gaze away from the empty space where the children had been a moment before and directing it back to his sister-in-law. "You're okay with money?"

"We've been fine, Linc. I keep trying to tell you that." Renee put a hand on his arm. "You don't need to take care of us anymore, not financially. We're doing fine. I'm working, and there was plenty of life insurance. We're doing okay, honest."

"It's the least I can do," he repeated.

Renee picked up the gift bags and tissue paper, and placed them on the coffee table. Then she sighed and sat back on the armchair. "Linc, stop bringing gifts. Stop sending us money." When he started to protest, she held up a hand. "The only thing the kids and I want is you. They need a male figure in their lives, someone who cares about them and will give them the kind of advice a mom can't."

"Renee, I'm no good with kids. I shouldn't—"

She leaned forward and put a hand on his knee, cutting off his sentence. "You should. And the kids, they just want to see their uncle. They don't expect you to be entertainer of the year. You've been here financially, and for that I'm grateful, but as an uncle—"

The sentence cut off, and he knew what she had left out. As an uncle, he had let the children down.

"I wanted to, but..." How could he explain that every time he saw the kids, it reminded him of the father they had lost? Of how he had been the reason for that loss? What kind of influence could he be, with all that hanging over him? And them?

Renee gave his arm a squeeze. "No more buts, Linc. I think the best thing for them, and for you, is for the three of you to spend time together. Nothing heals a broken heart like family. And, if you ask me, you're the one who needs healing the most out of all of us."

Molly had been home for a week already. She'd spent a ridiculous amount of time organizing drawers and closets that didn't need organizing, then going outside to her backyard garden, tending to her plants and adding new ones. In between, she walked Rocky, going farther each day both to clear her mind and keep her body moving, which the doctor said would be good in her second trimester. Sometimes she added her neighbor Mrs. Whitcomb's Papillion, Duke, because the older woman didn't get around as well as she used to, and the little dog loved playing with Rocky.

The applications she'd sent out before she left for Vegas had resulted in several callbacks, and she'd gone on two job interviews already, with one of them looking very promising for a teaching position next month. Ordinarily, she'd be excited about the new school year, getting to know her students, planning a new curriculum, designing fun bulletin boards and projects, but—

For some reason, her heart wasn't in the tasks like normal.

Jayne had done her best to cheer Molly up, inviting her out to dinner, to go shopping, and for a pedicure. Molly had gone along, hoping some friend time would alleviate the weight hanging on her shoulders.

It hadn't.

She called Alex and Serena, keeping in touch with them regularly through texts and phone messages, assuring them everything was fine. But whenever they asked about Linc, she evaded an answer.

Because she really didn't like the one she had.

She'd made it past the first trimester, and her morning sickness had stopped. Her obstetrician had told her everything looked good, and she should expect a March baby. It was time, she knew, to begin making plans. Once the school year got underway, she'd be too busy to do much more than sleep and create lesson plans, especially if she was working at a new school. The best thing to do was to get ready for the baby now.

She ducked into a baby store, and started wandering the aisles of gaily decorated cribs, filled with pastel blankets and piles of stuffed animals. A half-dozen couples milled about the store, talking excitedly with each other, exchanging kisses—

Making Molly feel more alone than she had five minutes ago. Her hand wandered to her stomach, just now starting to show, enough that she'd had to buy looser pants and a tunic top. Not maternity clothes yet, but something more comfortable. *Oh, baby*, she thought, *I wish your father was here*.

But he wasn't. And that situation wasn't going to change.

She turned, about to leave, when she saw Jayne walk into the store. Her face broke into a wide smile, and she welcomed her friend with a hug. "What are you doing here?"

"You mentioned that you were going shopping today for baby furniture, and I couldn't let you do that alone." Jayne grinned. "Where's the fun in that?"

"I'm so glad you're here." Tears threatened Molly's eyes, but she brushed them away before they could fall.

"None of that," Jayne said, wagging a good-natured finger at Molly. "This is supposed to be fun. So let's go pick out some furniture, okay?"

Molly nodded.

"You're going to be fine, Moll. You always are." Jayne

drew her friend into another hug, then they headed toward the cribs. They started with the basics, because it was easier to do that than to start with the reasons why Molly was shopping with her best friend—

Instead of with the father of her baby.

"How long are you going to be an idiot?"

Linc looked up to find Conner standing in his office, arms crossed over his chest. "Excuse me?"

"You're miserable. You're here. She's there. Get yourself on a plane and go see her."

Linc let out a breath. "It's complicated, Conner."

"When isn't life complicated? You think my relationship with my wife was a walk in the clouds from beginning to end? We had a rocky road ourselves. It goes with the territory." Conner crossed to Linc's desk and plopped into one of the visitors' chairs.

Linc glanced over at the dice clock that sat on his desk, the kitschy souvenir so out of place in the elegant office, but a constant reminder of his date with Molly, and those few times he'd slipped out of the responsibility yoke and had fun.

Molly. Linc had barely thought of anything but her in the last few days. He toyed with the clock, remembering that night at the aquarium, the day on the lake. She hadn't answered any of his calls, e-mails. She probably hated him.

Could he blame her?

"Speaking of Molly, have you seen the new software?" Linc asked Conner. After Molly had left, Linc had backed off from the project. It had been his idea from the beginning, but as soon as she'd walked out the door his enthusiasm seemed to have gone with her. He'd signed off on the program without looking at it, handing the project to his marketing team and allowing them to package it as they saw fit.

Conner rolled his eyes, but went along with the subject change. For a few minutes the two men talked about the spring launch planned for the program. "I know what you're doing."

"Trying to settle on a launch date." Linc scrolled through his calendar. "I'd like to get as early into the second quarter as possible, so we can have it on shelves before the end of the school year. We can offer it to parents as a summer—"

"I'm not discussing this with you anymore, not until you go look at the software yourself, Linc," Conner said, getting to his feet. "I think you'll be surprised at what you find, at the amazing things Molly did with the program. You know, you can't avoid this forever."

"I'm not avoiding anything. I've been busy."

"Now you're lying to yourself." Conner shook his head. "You know, for a little while there, I really thought you had changed. I was damned glad to see it, too, because if anyone in this company deserves to have it all, it's you."

He tossed a CD onto Linc's desk, then he walked out of Linc's office. The silver disk caught the light from above and winked back at Linc, with the logo for Inside Out Games dancing back in primary colors. Waiting for him to decide whether Conner was right.

Whether Linc had changed. Or was determined to stay exactly where he had been for most of his life.

CHAPTER TWELVE

ROCKY pulled on his leash, anxious to be home as dusk settled over San Diego. Molly inhaled, drawing in the fresh scent of the ocean, the salty tang in the air. She loved it here, always had. San Diego was such a stark contrast to Las Vegas. Here, she had friends, a richness of Mother Nature, a life.

Granted, she didn't have the one man she had been thinking about almost non-stop since she had gotten home, but she told herself she was okay with that.

That it hadn't broken her heart to leave Linc behind.

Because somewhere between the job offer and the kiss in the lake, Molly had done the one thing that she had vowed she wouldn't do.

She'd fallen in love with Linc. The man she knew was somewhere inside Lincoln Curtis, CEO. The man he kept setting aside, for whatever reason. Because of guilt over his brother's death, pressures from his job, or fear, perhaps, of getting close to someone else.

She'd had glimpses of the man she'd fallen for weeks ago, and whenever she had, her heart had become entangled more and more. That day she'd kidnapped him, she'd done more than just take Linc hostage.

She'd wrapped herself up in him forever, too. Ever since

she'd gotten home, she'd thought about him. Wondered where he was. What he was doing. Whether he ever thought about her or the baby.

He had thought about her. But not in the way she'd hoped.

He'd called. Left messages. Sent flowers. Cards.

She'd ignored them all. Because not a single one had said what she wanted them to say.

I want to make a family with you.

Until Linc said those magic words, she wanted nothing to do with him. She would move forward, just her and the baby, no matter how much it hurt, and no matter how many flowers he sent.

As she rounded the corner of Gull View Lane, she saw two things that seemed out of place.

A black town car sitting on the curb in front of her house. And her mother—

Talking to Lincoln Curtis.

Molly stopped walking, which made Rocky let out a yelp of protest, especially since he knew his favorite chew toy was only a few houses away. Linc was here?

And talking to her mother?

Joy exploded in her chest, but she tamped it down. A thousand different things could have brought Linc to San Diego. He could be here to talk about custody after the baby was born, or to ask her to work for him again. He could have come because she'd ignored all his other attempts at contact. The chances of him being here to see her—because he wanted to make their relationship work—

Were slim to none.

She started walking again, and in a couple of minutes had reached her drive, then her walkway. Her mother and Linc were so deeply engrossed in their conversation that they didn't notice her at first.

"You own your own company?" Cynthia asked Linc.

Oh, no. Her mother was on a roll now. Molly would undoubtedly hear all about how wonderful Linc was from her mother later. And trying to explain why Linc was a bad choice would likely go in one ear and out the other.

Had Linc told her mother that he was the father of the baby? Molly had only told her mother that it was a man she'd dated a few times. She'd not given her a name—because, knowing Cynthia, her mother would look the man up and have him at an altar before the end of the day. Her mother meant well, but she could be stubborn in the area of seeing her daughter get a happy ending.

"Yes, ma'am, I do. I own a software development company." Linc smiled at her. "In Las Vegas."

Cynthia made a little face. "That's awfully far away from here. You don't have a second office here in California?"

"No, but—" Rocky let out a bark, and Linc turned. When his gaze met Molly's, the friendly smile he'd given her mother expanded into a wider one. "Molly."

The soft way he said her name sent a quiver through her body. She hadn't realized until just then how much she had missed him. How endless the days apart had been. She'd thought she could forget him, that she could go up to him and tell him she had nothing to say to him—

She'd been wrong. One word out of his mouth, and she was already a goner. Oh, this was not good.

She started up the few porch steps. "Linc. What brings you all the way to San Diego?"

"He came to see you." Her mother lowered her voice to a whisper. "Make him dinner. Men love women who can cook, you know."

"Mom!"

Her mother cupped Molly's jaw and paused a moment to meet her daughter's eye. "I know I interfere, and I know I sometimes push you into the wrong direction. But I only want you to be happy, Molly."

"I know."

"He's a really nice man."

"Mom..."

"And I like him much better than Douglas." Cynthia cast a quick glance back in Linc's direction. "I can't even remember what I ever saw in Douglas. This one...he's a keeper."

Molly drew her mother into a one-armed hug. "Thanks for the advice. Now, please stop."

Her mother opened her mouth to say something else, then sighed instead. "Okay. I'm going to leave and go to my book club meeting."

"Book club meeting?"

"I took your advice and joined. I met the most amazing man there, too." Cynthia's eyes twinkled, as if she were a teenager all over again. "He's not a fan of Brontë, but I think I can change his mind." Her mother picked up her purse from the porch floor and swung it over her shoulder. For the first time Molly noticed Cynthia was wearing a dress, kitten heels and makeup—a big change from the last eighteen months. "Okay, I'm going now, so you two—" she glanced between Molly and Linc "—can be alone."

Molly rolled her eyes as her matchmaking mother got in her car and left, faster than she ever had before. Once Cynthia was gone, Molly turned to Linc. "I'm sorry about that. She tends to be—"

"A mom." Linc chuckled. "I don't mind."

"Do you want to come in? In case my other relatives

decide to stop by and put in their two cents over my personal life?"

"I'd like that." Linc followed her into her bungalow.

He still hadn't said why he was here. Molly tried to speculate, but gave up. She couldn't read anything in his face, and refused to hope. He knew when she left Las Vegas where she stood, and her non-responsiveness to his calls, e-mails and flowers had to be a sign that she still felt the same way.

"I'm sure it's not quite what you're used to," Molly said, immediately feeling the difference between her tiny house and the expansive penthouse apartment Linc owned. For the first time since she'd bought her cozy house, it seemed small and cramped.

"It's perfect," Linc said. "Reminds me of you. It's… comfortable. Like a fireplace on a cold day." He gestured toward the pictures, a quintet of oak frames of happier times that hung on the wall, images of her and her parents throughout the years. "Your mom and dad?"

She nodded. "My dad died a year and a half ago. He was a great man. Firefighter for twenty years, then became a middle school history teacher after he retired."

Linc turned toward her. "Is that why you went into teaching?"

She ran a hand down the frame that held her favorite picture of her father—him standing on the beach, holding Molly's hand when she'd been about six. They'd just finished building a sand castle, and her mother had snapped the photo just before the ocean reclaimed the sand. "Yes. He loved his job so much, it sounded like the perfect thing to do. I can still remember how proud he was the day I graduated from college with my teaching license."

"And you like teaching?"

"Yes. It's a rewarding job, though it has its frustrations, like any job. Still, I love my students. Love seeing them learn something new every day." She thought of telling him how much she had enjoyed working for him, too, about how rewarding that job had been, but she didn't. What if he offered her the job back? Then she'd have to admit to herself that she missed the daily opportunity to flex her creative muscles. That she'd been thinking about how much she wished she could go back to working at Curtis Systems—and not just to see Linc again.

"Did you enjoy working for me?" he asked, as if he had read her mind.

Now she couldn't duck out of answering. "Yes, I did."

"Why?"

"Would you like some lemonade? Iced tea?"

"Iced tea would be wonderful," he said, "and an answer, too."

She headed toward the kitchen. Linc followed behind and took a seat at her small maple kitchen table that sat at the end of the galley kitchen, facing the large picture window overlooking the back patio and her garden. His tall frame seemed to dominate the space, making her a hundred times more aware of him.

She reached in the refrigerator, pulled out the tea and poured it into a glass, then added several ice cubes. Trying to take her time, to delay the inevitable conversations. "Lemon?"

"Please."

A few more seconds while she sliced a lemon and plopped a thick wedge into his glass. Finally, when she could avoid him no longer, she crossed to the table, gave Linc his iced tea and sat down across from him.

"I saw the software, Molly."

"Oh." That was why he was here then. Because he was

upset with the job she had done. Here to tell her she needed to redo it, or give him back her salary. "I'm sorry if—"

"It was incredible. More than I had hoped for." He leaned across the table. His gaze met hers, deep blue eyes direct and powerful. "It was as if you read my mind."

"I simply went by your notes," she said, heat rising in her at Linc's continued attention. He had a way of looking at her—really looking at her—so that she felt like the only woman on earth. The only person he saw. His intensity pleased her, and scared her, because of how intoxicating such attention could be.

"No, you went *beyond* my notes. How did you do that?"

"I don't understand. I was...just doing my job, Linc. What you hired me for."

Rocky crossed to Linc, nosing at the stranger in the kitchen. Linc smiled, bent down and scratched Rocky behind the ears. Rocky let out a groan and pressed his little body to Linc's leg, wagging dog hair all over Linc's custom suit. Linc didn't seem to mind.

"You took what was an idea, a vision I had, and you made it something bigger than I had even dreamed, Molly. The ideas you had..." He shook his head. "For instance, I love that the children are encouraged, after they finish the grasshopper jumping game on screen, to go outside and look for real grasshoppers. To observe how they act, then come back to the program and put in their answers in order to get to the next level. You truly found a way to bridge the techno and natural worlds."

"I just tried to do what you said."

"No, you did more." A smile crossed his lips. "It's amazing. It's different. And it's going to take Curtis Systems in a whole new direction."

"I'm glad." She rose, unable to look at him any longer. Knowing that he was only here for the same thing as he always was.

Business.

Tears stung at the back of her eyes, and she turned toward the sink, to press the back of her hand to her face, keeping the tears from spilling out. Damn. Why did she keep hoping for something different?

For the impossible?

"So you came here to thank me?" she said, the words shredding her throat.

"Yes. And…"

She didn't turn around while she waited for him to finish the sentence. She couldn't.

"And to explain a few things."

She heard the scrape of the chair against the tile floor, and then Linc was behind her, the woodsy notes of his cologne teasing at her senses, tempting her to turn into his arms. She didn't. She held fast to her position against the sink, sure that if she faced him now, he'd read her every emotion—

And know she had fallen in love with him.

He put a hand on her shoulder, and gently turned her to face him. "Maybe if I tell you, you'll understand why I've made the choices I have. They may not be the right ones, but they seemed like the best ones, then and now."

"Okay." She owed him that, at least, and maybe then she would understand, and it would be easier to let him go. To forget him. Have a simple, civil relationship with their child between them.

He let out a long breath and ran a hand through his hair. "I told you that my brother died three years ago, but I didn't tell you everything." He swallowed, then went on.

"Marcus was born with a congenital heart disease. He had surgery to repair his heart valve when he was a baby, but the doctors said he would always be vulnerable to infections. He was supposed to be careful, take care of himself.

"Marcus just wasn't that kind of kid, though," Linc went on. "He was the daredevil, the one who would climb trees and go skiing. He wanted to have fun, not sit on the sidelines and worry about his heart. He always said our parents did enough worrying for him, that he could afford not to. So he never remembered to take his medication, or maybe just purposely forgot. I think he hated being reminded that he was 'different' or weak."

"I bet your parents worried about him a lot," Molly said, thinking like the mother she was about to become. How difficult that must have been for Linc's parents, having a child with a condition that required constant monitoring. They must have always been on edge.

He nodded, his face somber. "Constantly. When we lived at home, my mother was on top of his medication, his doctor's appointments. Then, when Marcus got out on his own, everyone thought he'd grow up and be responsible. But…" Linc shook his head. "He wasn't. He'd go skiing instead of going to the doctor's. Leave his pills behind. More than once he ended up in the hospital."

Molly waited, letting Linc tell the story in his own time.

"Around that time, my parents were in a car accident. It was…" He shook his head and crossed the room. He stopped in front of the large picture window. For a long time he stared out at Molly's garden, not saying anything at all. "My parents didn't make it. Dad died at the scene and Mom had too many internal injuries."

Molly placed a hand on Linc's back, communicating her sympathy by touch, wishing she could go back ten years in time and be with him then. "It must have been so hard on you. I know how difficult it was when my dad died, and I was older than you."

"I was eighteen. Marcus was sixteen." He heaved a sigh, and she could hear the weight of his grief in that sound. "The last thing my mother said to me was 'Watch out for your brother. Take care of him for us.' And that's what I did. Marcus and I made a deal—I'd stay on top of him, his pills, his appointments, and he could pretend to live a normal life. He never even told his wife about his heart." Linc let out a breath. "That, I didn't know. But with Marcus, that makes sense. He just wanted to be…normal. So I did enough worrying for both of us."

It all began to make sense now, the picture coming into focus for Molly, like a television that had suddenly been fixed. "Linc, you can't blame yourself for not being there when your brother died. Those things happen. They—"

He wheeled around. "I *can* damned well blame myself. Do you want to know where I was when my brother's heart started giving out? I was at a bar, getting drunk. Thinking I was having a good time. Relaxing for the first time in a decade."

"You were on vacation. You're supposed to relax."

"I was supposed to look out for my brother, Molly, not—"

He shook his head and turned back to the window. His shoulders hunched, and his back tensed.

"Not…what?"

"Not be sitting at that bar thinking it was about damned time my brother took care of me for once."

The words had slipped out of him in a whisper, raw and painful. He seemed to crumple into himself, as if the last string holding him up had been snipped. Or maybe it was simply the weight of his guilt, crushing him until he couldn't take the burden anymore.

"You can't blame yourself for that, Linc. Everyone—"

"No, Molly, I can. And I do. What kind of brother does that?"

"One who wanted his own life and deserved to have one," she said, wishing she could mend his broken heart with her own two hands. "Your parents wouldn't have wanted you to give up your own happiness to take care of your brother, and I doubt he wanted it, either."

"I should have been there. I should have…" His voice cracked, along with his composure.

Her arms went around him then, and she laid her head on his shoulder. "You did your best, Linc."

He shook his head.

"A congenital problem can attack someone at any time. Whether you're there or not."

"He called me. And I didn't answer." He heaved a breath. "Because I didn't want to work. Me, the one who always works. I wanted time off."

"That's not selfish, Linc." She came around him, until she had his face in her hands, and locked her gaze on his blue eyes. "It's human. And it's okay. You've always been the responsible one, and it's okay to not be that person once in a while. To live your own life."

He started to shake his head, tears glimmering in his eyes, but she kept repeating the words, telling him over and over that what he did was okay, that it wasn't a sin, forgiving him for the people who couldn't.

Finally, Linc stopped, and she could see him trying to accept the fact that he had done nothing more than be a regular person. "If I'd just answered the phone, maybe I could have…"

"Maybe," she said softly. "And maybe it wouldn't have made any difference at all. Either way, do you think your brother would want you to spend the rest of your life feeling guilty?"

He let out a long breath. "No."

She could hear in his voice, though, that it didn't matter. Linc still felt as if he had to pay a penance for a crime he hadn't committed out of anything other than simple human nature. "You remember what you told me about why you liked those rock outcroppings so much at Lake Mead?" she said.

"The rocks? What do they have to do with anything?"

"Because they don't change, you said. They stay the same, year after year. They don't move, they don't go anywhere, they don't grow." She dropped her hands from his face. "You're like those rocks, Linc. You haven't moved or grown or changed in all the years since your brother died. Except for that one night we had together. Then you were the man you could be, if only you'd stop standing still."

"Molly, you don't understand—"

A long, slow and sad smile slid across her face. "I do, Linc. All you have to do is decide that you're tired of being a rock. And start being a person again. Allow yourself to live." She reached up and cupped his jaw. "Stop paying for a crime you didn't commit."

"And what? Be a father? God, Molly, you have no idea how much I want to be. But what if…?" He glanced down at her belly, at the small swell beneath her pale pink tunic top. "What if I make the same mistakes? What if our baby is born with the same problems my brother had?"

"And what if the baby isn't? There are no guarantees in parenthood, Linc. You just do the best you can."

"Like you're doing."

She nodded, feeling the sting of tears when she thought of the long, lonely road ahead. Of raising their child without him. "I'm trying."

"Then why did you leave?"

She let out a gust and turned away. "Why would I stay? To be another line in your schedule? To have the baby end up on your 'To Do' list? No, Linc. I want the whole thing. The family. The husband. All of us sitting around the Christmas tree opening presents and then debating whether we want roast beef or ham for dinner."

"For someone who wants it all, you've done a good job of trying to avoid a commitment yourself."

"What do you mean? I've done nothing but try to connect with you. I came all the way to Vegas—"

"Yet you didn't tell me the truth until you had to."

She wrapped her hands around the cold glass of iced tea. "Because that's not the kind of thing you spring on someone. And you made it clear from the beginning that you were not the family man type."

"You kept trying to get me to open up, but you wouldn't do the same with me."

"I did. I…" Her voice trailed off as she realized that she had kept much of herself back in those weeks she'd been in Vegas. Thinking she was being so smart, keeping her heart protected.

Had it been smart after all? Look where she'd ended up—alone again.

He shook his head. "We're two of a kind, aren't we, Molly? Both of us wanting so much to have it all, but being too afraid to really try?"

"That may be true, Linc, but for me, fear or not, I don't have a choice." She met his gaze, and her spine straightened as a strength she hadn't realized she had infused her. "You can walk away and bury yourself in work again, if you want, but I'm going to stay right here. And have our baby."

Linc sat in the back of the town car for a long time. Saul tried to engage him in conversation twice, but gave up when he only got one-word answers from his boss. Finally, Linc opened the back door himself and got out, waving Saul off. "I'll be back in a little while."

He wandered down the concrete ramp, then stopped just shy of where the cement ended and the sand began. He bent down, unlaced his thousand-dollar shoes, tucked them and his socks under his arm, then started forward. His bare feet sank into the sand of the beach, a softer, prettier and whiter sand than the one at Lake Mead, but to him it felt as if he was back at the Las Vegas lake with Molly.

He walked the San Diego beach for a good half hour, watching the surf, the kids darting in and out of the water, the gulls diving for crumbs and fish, then turned around and headed halfway back to where the car was parked. Long enough to clear his head, come to some decisions.

And find a good place to sit. A forgotten Adirondack chair with a built-in umbrella, one of those nice wooden ones hotels rented out to their customers, then tucked away at the end of the day.

Linc sat down, pulled out a pen—

And finally let go of the past.

"He's right," Molly said, thinking of what Linc had said to her before he'd left. "I hate that."

Alex and Serena, their two faces pressed together so they could both be seen in Alex's Web cam, laughed. "Then find him and tell him," Alex said.

Molly sighed. "But what if it doesn't work out? What if I make another mistake?"

"Falling in love is about taking a leap of faith, Molly. Sometimes it works out, and sometimes it doesn't, but when it does…" A wide smile spread across Alex's face, and once again a stab of envy ran through Molly. "It's wonderful."

She could have that, Molly realized. If only she'd let go and trust. Allow Linc into her heart.

"You deserve a happy ending," Serena said. "A Prince Charming of your own."

Molly smiled. "Thanks, guys. Every time I talk to you two or Jayne, I always feel better."

Alex laughed. "That's because we're the voice of reason. Maybe not always for ourselves, but always for other people."

Molly joined in their laughter. The three of them chatted a little while longer about their lives, then disconnected. She sat back in her desk chair for a long time after the Web cam turned off, thinking about what Alex had said.

Take a leap of faith with Linc. Trust in him—but most of all in herself—that the second time around she had made a better choice.

Could she do that?

Her doorbell rang. Rocky scrambled to his feet and began to bark, little non-ferocious yips that wouldn't have scared off anyone, but he thought sounded like a guard dog. Molly gave him an appreciative pat on the head, then crossed to open the door.

Linc stood on her doorstep. Again.

"I thought you went back to Vegas."

"I can't." He grinned.

"Why?"

"Everything I want is here. In San Diego."

Her heart sang, but she tamped down the feeling. They'd been here before, just a couple hours ago. "Here?"

"I went down to the beach," he said. "Walked for a long time. In fact, I think I still have sand in my shoes."

She laughed. "You? Walked on the beach?"

He nodded. "I think someone I know called it playing hooky."

"That I did."

He reached up and caught a tendril of her hair, and she held her breath as he let it slip through his hand, slow, sensual, making her melt with desire. "You were right. I've let guilt run my life long enough."

"I'm glad to hear that." She wanted to back up, to escape his touch. He was here to say goodbye, she was sure of it. And she just couldn't do that twice.

Linc released her, then bent down and retrieved something from the table on her porch. "While I was there, I finished this. For you. For the baby."

He handed her the *Memories for Your Baby* journal. Molly took it, then opened the book, and found the pages inside filled with Linc's neat script. Everything from his favorite color to his earliest childhood memory, written down, in detail.

"You...you did it." Each page revealed something more about Linc, something she hadn't known before. Another piece of his soul, his heart.

Linc's entire self, written in the pages of their baby's journal. She ran a palm over the fresh ink, feeling more connected to him at that moment than ever before.

"It needs something more, though."

"What? I mean, it looks like you've filled in everything you could. I'm just amazed, Linc, I never thought—"

"It needs your stories, Molly. You never filled in your pages, either."

She stopped and looked up at him. She hadn't, had she? All this time she'd been concentrating on garnering information about Linc. She'd completely forgotten about the mom pages.

"When you do, I want to read them," Linc said, taking a step closer to her, closing the gap until she wasn't sure where she ended and he began. "I want to know everything about you, Molly. What kind of eggs you like in the morning. If you sleep on the right side of the bed or the left. If you like romantic movies or thrillers."

What was he saying? Had she heard him right? "You…but…why?"

A grin curved up his face. "Because if I'm going to move my business to San Diego, I want to be sure."

Move his business to San Diego? The words swam in Molly's head. Had she heard him right? "Be sure about what?"

He reached up and cupped her jaw, running his thumb over her bottom lip. "I want to be sure that I know everything I can about the woman I want to marry."

She blinked. "Marry? Did you just say you want to marry me?"

"I love you, Molly. I've loved you since I met you that night in the bar. I love the way you take chances, the way you have this amazing mix of sweet and sassy, even the way you boss me around sometimes." He chuckled.

"You…you do? But…" She couldn't even form the words, just vague questions.

"The more I wrote in that journal, the more I realized I wanted to make new memories. With you. With our baby. I didn't want to look back at my life in five years or ten or twenty and just see empty pages, ones that didn't have you and our baby in them. Over the last week, I've spent a lot of time with my niece and nephew and it made me realize how much I want to spend time with my own child. How much I don't want to miss out on those years."

She stood there, dumbfounded.

"You were right," he went on, "I was like those rocks at the lake. And if I kept on going the way I was, my life would be as cold and hard as them." He pressed a kiss to her forehead, then another to her cheek. "You made this rock move and change. And, to be honest, it was about damned time. So marry me and let's be a family."

Joy took wing in her heart. He loved her? Wanted to marry her? "Linc, I…I don't know what to say."

"Then just say yes." He kissed her other cheek, then her lips. "I've spent too many years using work to fill the hole in my heart when all I had to do was look—" at this his blue eyes connected with hers "—at you."

Her heart melted, her arms stole around Linc, and she curved into him. "Oh, Linc, I love you, too. And, yes—yes, I'll marry you."

A smile broke across his face, bloomed in his blue eyes. His hand slipped between them, to rest on her abdomen. "Then I think we need to find a pen."

"A pen? Why?"

"Because there's a page in the baby book for 'When Your Parents Fell in Love'." He kissed Molly, long and sweet and sure, then pulled back. "And I think that moment is now."

Molly smiled up at Linc—not Lincoln Curtis, but Linc, the man she had met, the man she had, indeed, fallen in love with—and smiled. "And what will we put? That we had a one-night stand, one crazy night in Vegas, and it turned into something more?"

He shook his head. "No. We'll put the truth. That one night I met you and I loved you. But I just didn't realize it until love came back and kidnapped me."

Molly leaned into Linc, fitting perfectly against his chest, and felt his arms wrap around her. "That," she said, "is exactly what happened to me, too."

Coming Next Month

Available August 10, 2010

LARGER-PRINT BOOKS!
GET 2 FREE LARGER-PRINT NOVELS PLUS
2 FREE GIFTS!

From the Heart, For the Heart

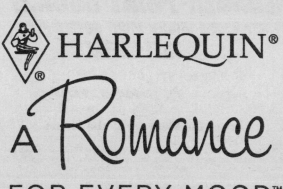

HARLEQUIN®

A Romance

FOR EVERY MOOD™

Spotlight on

— Heart & Home —

Heartwarming romances
where love can happen
right when you least expect it.

See the next page to enjoy a sneak peek
from Harlequin® American Romance®,
a Heart and Home series.

CATHHHAR10

*Five hunky Texas single fathers—five stories from
Cathy Gillen Thacker's* LONE STAR DADS *miniseries.
Here's an excerpt from the latest,* THE MOMMY PROPOSAL
from Harlequin American Romance.

"I hear you work miracles," Nate Hutchinson drawled. Brooke Mitchell had just stepped into his lavishly appointed office in downtown Fort Worth, Texas.

"Sometimes, I do." Brooke smiled and took the sexy financier's hand in hers, shook it briefly.

"Good." Nate looked her straight in the eye. "Because I'm in need of a home makeover—fast. The son of an old friend is coming to live with me."

She was still tingling from the feel of his warm palm. "Temporarily or permanently?"

"If all goes according to plan, I'll adopt Landry by summer's end."

Brooke had heard the founder of Nate Hutchinson Financial Services was eligible, wealthy and generous to a fault. She hadn't known he was in the market for a family, but she supposed she shouldn't be surprised. But Brooke had figured a man as successful and handsome as Nate would want one the old-fashioned way. *Not that this was any of her business...*

"So what's the child like?" she asked crisply, trying not to think how the marine-blue of Nate's dress shirt deepened the hue of his eyes.

"I don't know." Nate took a seat behind his massive antique mahogany desk. He relaxed against the smooth leather of the chair. "I've never met him."

"Yet you've invited this kid to live with you permanently?"

"It's complicated. But I'm sure it's going to be fine."

Obviously Nate Hutchinson knew as little about teenage

boys as he did about decorating. But that wasn't her problem.
Finding a way to do the assignment without getting the least
bit emotionally involved was.

Find out how a young boy brings Nate and Brooke
together in THE MOMMY PROPOSAL,
coming August 2010 from Harlequin American Romance.

ROMANTIC
SUSPENSE

Sparked by Danger, Fueled by Passion.

SILHOUETTE ROMANTIC SUSPENSE BRINGS YOU AN ALL-NEW COLTONS OF MONTANA STORY!

FBI agent Jake Pierson is determined to solve his case, even if it means courting and using the daughter of a murdered informant. Mary Walsh hates liars and, now that Jake has fallen deeply in love, he is afraid to tell her the truth. But the truth is not the only thing out there to hurt Mary…

Be part of the romance and suspense in

Covert Agent's Virgin Affair
by
LINDA CONRAD

Available August 2010 where books are sold.

Visit Silhouette Books at www.eHarlequin.com

SRS27690

Love Inspired.
HISTORICAL
INSPIRATIONAL HISTORICAL ROMANCE

Bestselling author

JILLIAN HART

brings readers
a new heartwarming story in

Patchwork Bride

Meredith Worthington is returning to
Angel Falls, Montana, to follow her dream
of becoming a teacher. And perhaps get to know
Shane Connelly, the intriguing new wrangler on
her father's ranch. Shane can't resist her charm
even though she reminds him of everything he'd like
to forget. But will love have time to blossom before
she discovers the secret he's been hiding all along?

Available in August
wherever books are sold.

Steeple
Hill®
LIH82841

www.SteepleHill.com